£1·50

# THE QUEEN OF AIR AND DARKNESS AND OTHER STORIES

# The Queen of Air and Darkness and Other Stories

POUL ANDERSON

NEW ENGLISH LIBRARY
TIMES MIRROR

To Lin and Noel Carter

First published in the USA by Signet Books, The New American Library in 1973
© 1973 by Poul Anderson

These stories were first published and copyrighted as follows:

In *The Magazine of Fantasy and Science Fiction*: 'Time Lag', January, 1961; 'The Queen of Air and Darkness', April, 1971. Copyright © 1961 and 1971, respectively, by Mercury Press, Inc.

In *Analog Science Fact/Science Fiction*: 'In the Shadow', March, 1967; 'The Alien Enemy', December, 1968 – both under the pseudonym Michael Karageorge. Copyright © 1967 and 1968, respectively, by The Condé Nast Publications, Inc.

In *Boys' Life*: 'The Faun', September, 1968. Copyright © 1968 by the Boy Scouts of America.

In *Orbit 1*: 'Home', under the title 'The Disinherited'. Copyright © 1966 by Berkley Publishing Corporation.

*

FIRST NEL PAPERBACK EDITION JUNE 1977

*

*NEL Books are published by*
*New English Library Limited from Barnard's Inn, Holborn, London EC1N 2JR*
*Made and printed in Great Britain by Hunt Barnard Printing Ltd., Aylesbury, Bucks.*

45003161 6

# CONTENTS

# FOREWORD

The stories in this book are not related in the sense of projecting a single history of the future. What they do have in common is an idea.

Or maybe it is a question. How much of the universe does science *as we know it* open to us?

We would be rash indeed to claim that we, today, understand everything between the heart of the atom and the farthest of the galaxies. Our first small probings and ventures beyond Earth have already given us more riddles than answers. Extrasensory perception and other peculiar phenomena are becoming respectable fields for research. The professional journals now publish speculations which make fiction look tame. (Thus, the concept of 'shadow matter' first appeared as a suggestion by K. Nishijima and M. H. Saffouri in *Physical Review Letters*, February 8, 1965.) You will find this attitude implicit in these tales.

But you will find nothing which most twentieth-century physicists would flatly call impossible, such as travel at speeds faster than light's. I would like to believe that that achievement, and others, will someday after all be ours. But the point is that we need not have unbounded capabilities in order to have an unbounded future.

The fact must include evil as well as good, error as well as wisdom. Some stories are therefore dark. The rest are brighter. In the long run – probably – the fate of humankind lies in what humans do.

– P. A.

# THE QUEEN OF AIR
# AND DARKNESS

The last glow of the last sunset would linger almost until mid-winter. But there would be no more day, and the northlands rejoiced. Blossoms opened, flamboyance on firethorn trees, steelflowers rising blue from the brok and rainplant that cloaked all hills, shy whiteness of kiss-me-never down in the dales. Flitteries darted among them on iridescent wings; a crownbuck shook his horns and bugled through warmth and flower odors. Between horizons the sky deepened from purple to sable. Both moons were aloft, nearly full, shining frosty on leaves and molten on waters. The shadows they made were blurred by an aurora, a great blowing curtain of light across half heaven. Behind it the earliest stars had come out.

A boy and a girl sat on Wolund's Barrow just under the dolmen it upbore. Their hair, which streamed halfway down their backs, showed startlingly forth, bleached as it was by summer. Their bodies, still dark from that season, merged with earth and bush and rock; for they wore only garlands. He played on a bone flute and she sang. They had lately become lovers. Their age was about sixteen, but they did not know this, considering themselves Outlings and thus indifferent to time, remembering little or nothing of how they had once dwelt in the lands of men.

His notes piped cold around her voice:
'Cast a spell,
weave it well
of dust and dew
and night and you.'
A brook by the grave mound, carrying moonlight down to a hill-hidden river, answered with its rapids. A flock of hellbats passed black beneath the aurora.

A shape came bounding over Cloudmoor. It had two arms and two legs, but the legs were long and claw-footed and feathers covered it to the end of a tail and broad wings. The face was half-human, dominated by its eyes. Had Ayoch been able to stand wholly erect, he would have reached to the boy's shoulder.

The girl rose. 'He carries a burden,' she said. Her vision was not meant for twilight like that of a northland creature born, but she had learned how to use every sign her senses gave her. Besides the fact that ordinarily a pook would fly, there was a heaviness to his haste.

'And he comes from the south.' Excitement jumped in the boy, sudden as a green flame that went across the constellation Lyrth. He sped down the mound. 'Ohoi, Ayoch!' he called. 'Me here, Mistherd!'

'And Shadow-of-a-Dream,' the girl laughed, following.

The pook halted. He breathed louder than the soughing in the growth around him. A smell of bruised yerba lifted where he stood.

'Well met in winterbirth,' he whistled. 'You can help me bring this to Carheddin.'

He held out what he bore. His eyes were yellow lanterns above. It moved and whimpered.

'Why, a child,' Mistherd said.

'Even as you were, my son, even as you were. Ho, ho, what a snatch!' Ayoch boasted. 'They were a score in yon camp by Fallowwood, armed, and besides watcher engines they had big ugly dogs aprowl while they slept. I came from above, however, having spied on them till I knew that a handful of dazedust – '

'The poor thing,' Shadow-of-a-Dream took the boy and held him to her small breasts. 'So full of sleep yet, aren't you, littleboo?' Blindly, he sought a nipple. She smiled through the veil of her hair. 'No, I am still too young, and you already too old. But come, when you wake in Carheddin under the mountain you shall feast.'

'Yo-ah,' said Ayoch very softly. 'She is abroad and has heard and seen. She comes.' He crouched down, wings folded. After a moment Mistherd knelt, and then Shadow-of-a-Dream, though she did not let go the child.

The Queen's tall form blocked off the moons. For a while she regarded the three and their booty. Hill and moor sounds withdrew from their awareness until it seemed they could hear the northlights hiss.

At last Ayoch whispered, 'Have I done well, Starmother?'

'If you stole a babe from a camp full of engines,' said the beautiful voice, 'then they were folk out of the far south who may not endure it as meekly as yeomen.'

'But what can they do, Snowmaker?' the pook asked. 'How can they track us?'

Mistherd lifted his head and spoke in pride. 'Also, now they too have felt the awe of us.'

'And he is cuddly dear,' Shadow-of-a-Dream said. 'And we need more like him, do we not, Lady Sky?'

'It had to happen in some twilight,' agreed she who stood above. 'Take him onward and care for him. By this sign,' which she made, 'is he claimed for the Dwellers.'

Their joy was freed. Ayoch cartwheeled over the ground till he reached a shiverleaf. There he swarmed up the trunk and out on a limb, perched half hidden by unrestful pale foliage, and crowded. Boy and girl bore the child toward Carheddin at an easy distance-devouring lope which let him pipe and her sing:

'Wahaii, wahaii!
Wayala, laii!
Wing on the wind
high over heaven,
shrilly shrieking,
rush with the rainspears,
tumble through tumult.
drift to the moonhoar trees and the dream-heavy
    shadows beneath them,
and rock in, be one with the clinking wavelets of lakes where
    the starbeams drown.'

As she entered, Barbro Cullen felt, through all grief and fury, stabbed by dismay. The room was unkempt. Journals, tapes, reels, codices, file boxes, bescribbled papers were piled on every table. Dust filmed most shelves and corners. Against one wall stood a laboratory setup, microscope and analytical equipment. She recognized it as compact and efficient, but it was not what you would expect in an office, and it gave the air a faint chemical reek. The rug was threadbare, the furniture shabby.

This was her final chance?

Then Eric Sherrinford approached. 'Good day, Mrs Cullen,' he said. His tone was crisp, his handclasp firm. His faded grip-suit didn't bother her. She wasn't inclined to fuss about her own appearance except on special occasions. (And would she ever again have one, unless she got back Jimmy?) What she observed was a cat's personal neatness.

A smile radiated in crow's feet from his eyes. 'Forgive my

bachelor housekeeping. On Beowulf we have – we had, at any rate – machines for that, so I never acquired the habit myself, and I don't want a hireling disarranging my tools. More convenient to work out of my apartment than keep a separate office. Won't you be seated?'

'No. thanks. I couldn't,' she mumbled.

'I understand. But if you'll excuse me, I function best in a relaxed position.'

He jackknifed into a lounger. One long shank crossed the other knee. He drew forth a pipe and stuffed it from a pouch. Barbro wondered why he took tobacco in so ancient a way. Wasn't Beowulf supposed to have the up-to-date equipment that they still couldn't afford to build on Roland? Well, of course old customs might survive anyhow. They generally did in colonies, she remembered reading. People had moved starward in the hope of preserving such outmoded things as their mother tongues or constitutional government or rational-technological civilization . . .

Sherrinford pulled her up from the confusion of her weariness: 'You must give me the details of your case, Mrs Cullen. You've simply told me that your son was kidnapped and your local constabulary did nothing. Otherwise I know just a few obvious facts, such as your being widowed rather than divorced; and you're the daughter of outwayers in Olga Ivanoff Land who, nevertheless, kept in close telecommunication with Christmas Landing; and you're trained in one of the biological professions; and you had several years' hiatus in field work until recently you started again.'

She gaped at the high-cheeked, beak-nosed, black-haired and gray-eyed countenance. His lighter made a *scrit* and a flare which seemed to fill the room. Quietness dwelt on this height above the city, and winter dusk was seeping in through the windows. 'How in cosmos do you know that?' she heard herself exclaim.

He shrugged and fell into the lecturer's manner for which he was notorious. 'My work depends on noticing details and fitting them together. In more than a hundred years on Roland, the people, tending to cluster according to their origins and thought-habits, have developed regional accents. You have a trace of the Olgan burr, but you nasalize your vowels in the style of this area, though you live in Portolondon. That suggests steady childhood exposure to metropolitan speech. You were part of Matsuyama's expedition, you told me, and took your boy along.

They wouldn't have allowed any ordinary technician to do that; hence you had to be valuable enough to get away with it. The team was conducting ecological research; therefore you must be in the life sciences. For the same reason, you must have had previous field experience. But your skin is fair, showing none of the leatheriness one gets from prolonged exposure to this sun. Accordingly, you must have been mostly indoors for a good while before you went on your ill-fated trip. As for widowhood – you never mentioned a husband to me, but you have had a man whom you thought so highly of that you still wear both the wedding and the engagement ring he gave you.'

Her sight blurred and stung. The last of those words had brought Tim back, huge, ruddy, laughterful and gentle. She must turn from this other person and stare outward. 'Yes,' she achieved saying, 'you're right.'

The apartment occupied a hilltop above Christmas Landing. Beneath it the city dropped away in walls, roofs, archaistic chimneys and lamplit streets, goblin lights of human-piloted vehicles, to the harbor, the sweep of Venture Boy, ships bound to and from the Sunward Islands and remoter regions of the Boreal Ocean, which glimmered like mercury in the afterglow of Charlemagne. Oliver was swinging rapidly higher, a mottled orange disc a full degree wide; closer to the zenith which it could never reach, it would shine the color of ice. Alde, half the seeming size, was a thin slow crescent near Sirius, which she remembered was near Sol, but you couldn't see Sol without a telescope –

'Yes,' she said around the pain in her throat, 'my husband is about four years dead. I was carrying our first child when he was killed by a stampeding monocerus. We'd been married three years before. Met while we were both at the University – 'casts from School Central can only supply a basic education, you know – we founded our own team to do ecological studies under contract – you know – can a certain area be settled while maintaining a balance of nature, what crops will grow, what hazards, that sort of question – Well, afterward I did lab work for a fisher co-op in Portolondon. But the monotony, the . . . shut-in-ness . . . was eating me away. Professor Matsuyama offered me a position on the team he was organizing to examine Commissioner Hauch Land. I thought, God help me, I thought Jimmy – Tim wanted him named James, once the tests showed it'd be a boy, after his own father and because of "Timmy and Jimmy" and – Oh, I thought Jimmy could safely

13

come along. I couldn't bear to leave him behind for months, not at his age. We could make sure he'd never wander out of camp. What could hurt him inside it? *I* had never believed those stories about the Outlings stealing human children. I supposed parents were trying to hide from themselves the fact they'd been careless, they'd let a kid get lost in the woods or attacked by a pack of satans or – Well, I learned better, Mr Sherrinford. The guard robots were evaded and the dogs were drugged and when I woke, Jimmy was gone.'

He regarded her through the smoke from his pipe. Barbro Engdahl Cullen was a big woman of thirty or so (Rolandic years, he reminded himself, ninety-five percent of Terrestrial, not the same as Beowulfan years), broad-shouldered, long-legged, full-breasted, supple of stride; her face was wide, straight nose, straightforward hazel eyes, heavy but mobile mouth; her hair was reddish-brown, cropped below the ears, her voice husky, her garment a plain street robe. To still the writhing of her fingers, he asked skeptically, 'Do you now believe in the Outlings?'

'No. I'm just not so sure as I was.' She swung about with half a glare for him. 'And we have found traces.'

'Bits of fossils,' he nodded. 'A few artifacts of a neolithic sort. But apparently ancient, as if the makers died ages ago. Intensive search has failed to turn up any real evidence for their survival.'

'How intensive can search be, in a summer-stormy, winter-gloomy wilderness around the North Pole?' she demanded. 'When we are, how many, a million people on an entire planet, half of us crowded into this one city?'

'And the rest crowding this one habitable continent,' he pointed out.

'Arctica covers five million square kilometers,' she flung back. 'The Arctic Zone proper covers a fourth of it. We haven't the industrial base to establish satellite monitor stations, build aircraft we can trust in those parts, drive roads through the damned darklands and establish permanent bases and get to know them and tame them. Good Christ, generations of lonely outwaymen told stories about Graymantle, and the beast was never seen by a proper scientist till last year!'

'Still, you continue to doubt the reality of the Outlings?'

'Well, what about a secret cult among humans, born of isolation and ignorance, lairing in the wilderness, stealing children when they can for – ' She swallowed. Her head drooped. 'But you're supposed to be the expert.'

14

'From what you told me over the visiphone, the Portolondon constabulary questions the accuracy of the report your group made, thinks the lot of you were hysterical, claims you must have omitted a due precaution and the child toddled away and was lost beyond your finding.'

His dry words pried the horror out of her. Flushing, she snapped: 'Like any settler's kid? No. I didn't simply yell. I consulted Data Retrieval. A few too many such cases are recorded for accident to be a very plausible explanation. And shall we totally ignore the frightened stories about reappearances? But when I went back to the constabulary with my facts, they brushed me off. I suspect that was not entirely because they're undermanned. I think they're afraid too. They're recruited from country boys; and Portolondon lies near the edge of the unknown.'

Her energy faded. 'Roland hasn't got any central police force,' she finished drably. 'You're my last hope.'

The man puffed smoke into twilight, with which it blent, before he said in a kindlier voice than hitherto: 'Please don't make it a high hope, Mrs Cullen. I'm the solitary private investigator on this world, having no resources beyond myself, and a newcomer to boot.'

'How long have you been here?'

'Twelve years. Barely time to get a little familiarity with the relatively civilized coastlands. You settlers of a century or more – what do you, even, know about Arctica's interior?'

Sherrinford sighed. 'I'll take the case, charging no more than I must, mainly for the sake of the experience,' he said. 'But only if you'll be my guide and assistant, however painful it will be for you.'

'Of course! I dreaded waiting idle. Why me, though?'

'Hiring someone else as well qualified would be prohibitively expensive, on a prisoner planet where every hand has a thousand urgent tasks to do. Besides, you have motive. And I'll need that. I, who was born on another world altogether strange to this one, itself altogether strange to Mother Earth, I am too dauntingly aware of how handicapped we are.'

Night gathered upon Christmas Landing. The air stayed mild, but glimmer-lit tendrils of fog, sneaking through the streets, had a cold look, and colder yet was the aurora where it shuddered between the moons. The woman drew closer to the man in this darkening room, surely not aware that she did, until

15

he switched on a fluropanel. The same knowledge of Roland's aloneness was in both of them.

One light-year is not much as galactic distances go. You could walk it in about 270 million years, beginning at the middle of the Permian Era, when dinosaurs belonged to the remote future, and continuing to the present day when spaceships cross even greater reaches. But stars in our neighborhood average some nine light-years apart; and barely one percent of them have planets which are man-habitable; and speeds are limited to less than that of radiation. Scant help is given by relativistic time contraction and suspended animation en route. These make the journeys seem short; but history meanwhile does not stop at home.

Thus voyages from sun to sun will always be few. Colonists will be those who have extremely special reasons for going. They will take along germ plasm for exogenetic cultivation of domestic plants and animals – and of human infants, in order that population can grow fast enough to escape death through genetic drift. After all, they cannot rely on further immigration. Two or three times a century, a ship may call from some other colony. (Not from Earth. Earth has long ago sunk into alien concerns.) Its place of origin will be an old settlement. The young ones are in no position to build and man interstellar vessels.

Their very survival, let alone their eventual modernization, is in doubt. The founding fathers have had to take what they could get, in a universe not especially designed for man.

Consider, for example, Roland. It is among the rare happy finds, a world where humans can live, breathe, eat the food, drink the water, walk unclad if they choose, sow their crops, pasture their beasts, dig their mines, erect their homes, raise their children and grandchildren. It is worth crossing three quarters of a light-century to preserve certain dear values and strike new roots into the soil of Roland.

But the star Charlemagne is of type F9, forty percent brighter than Sol, brighter still in the treacherous ultraviolet and wilder still in the wind of charged particles that seethes from it. The planet has an eccentric orbit. In the middle of the short but furious northern summer, which includes periastron, total isolation is more than double what Earth gets; in the depth of the long northern winter, it is barely less than Terrestrial average.

Native life is abundant everywhere. But lacking elaborate machinery, not economically possible to construct for more than a few specialists, man can only endure the high latitudes. A ten-

16

degree axial tilt, together with the orbit, means that the northern part of the Arctican continent spends half its year in unbroken sunlessness. Around the South Pole lies an empty ocean.

Other differences from Earth might superficially seem more important. Roland has two moons, small but close, to evoke clashing tides. It rotates once in thirty-two hours, which is endlessly, subtly disturbing to organisms evolved through gigayears of a quicker rhythm. The weather patterns are altogether unterrestrial. The globe is a mere 9500 kilometers in diameter; its surface gravity is $0.42 \times 980$ cm/sec$^2$; the sea-level air pressure is slightly above one Earth atmosphere. (For actually Earth is the freak, and man exists because a cosmic accident blew away most of the gas that a body its size ought to have kept, as Venus has done.)

However, *Homo* can truly be called *sapiens* when he practices his speciality of being unspecialized. His repeated attempts to freeze himself into an all-answering pattern or culture or ideology, or whatever he has named it, have repeatedly brought ruin. Give him the pragmatic business of making his living and he will usually do rather well. He adapts, within broad limits.

These limits are set by such factors as his need for sunlight and his being, necessarily and forever, a part of the life that surrounds him and a creature of the spirit within.


Portolondon thrust docks, boats, machinery, warehouses into the Gulf of Polaris. Behind them huddled the dwellings of its 5000 permanent inhabitants: concrete walls, storm shutters, high-peaked tile roofs. The gaiety of their paint looked forlorn amidst lamps; this town lay past the Arctic Circle.

Nevertheless Sherrinford remarked, 'Cheerful place, eh? The kind of thing I came to Roland looking for.'

Barbro made no reply. The days in Christmas Landing, while he made his preparations, had drained her. Gazing out the dome of the taxi that was whirring them downtown from the hydrofoil that brought them, she supposed he meant the lushness of forest and meadows along the road, brilliant hues and phosphorescence of flowers in gardens, clamor of wings overhead. Unlike Terrestrial flora in cold climates, Arctican vegetation spends every daylit hour in frantic growth and energy storage. Not till summer's fever gives place to gentle winter does it bloom and fruit; and estivating animals rise from their dens and migratory birds come home.

The view was lovely, she had to admit: beyond the trees, a

spaciousness climbing toward remote heights, silvery-gray under a moon, an aurora, the diffuse radiance from a sun just below the horizon.

Beautiful as a hunting satan, she thought, and as terrible. That wilderness had stolen Jimmy. She wondered if she would at least be given to find his little bones and take them to his father.

Abruptly she realized that she and Sherrinford were at their hotel and that he had been speaking of the town. Since it was next in size after the capital, he must have visited here often before. The streets were crowded and noisy; signs flickered, music blared from shops, taverns, restaurants, sports centers, dance halls; vehicles were jammed down to molasses speed; the several-stories-high office buildings stood aglow. Portolondon linked an enormous hinterland to the outside world. Down the Gloria River came timber rafts, ores, harvest of farms whose owners were slowly making Rolandic life serve them, meat and ivory and furs gathered by rangers in the mountains beyond Troll Scarp. In from the sea came coastwise freighters, the fishing fleet, produce of the Sunward Islands, plunder of whole continents further south where bold men adventured. It clanged in Portolondon, laughed, blustered, swaggered, connived, robbed, preached, guzzled, swilled, toiled, dreamed, lusted, built, destroyed, died, was born, was happy, angry, sorrowful, greedy, vulgar, loving, ambitious, human. Neither the sun's blaze elsewhere nor the half year's twilight here – wholly night around midwinter – was going to stay man's hand.

Or so everybody said.

Everybody except those who had settled in the darklands. Barbro used to take for granted that they were evolving curious customs, legends, and superstitions, which would die when the outway had been completely mapped and controlled. Of late, she had wondered. Perhaps Sherrinford's hints, about a change in his own attitude brought about by his preliminary research, were responsible.

Or perhaps she just needed something to think about besides how Jimmy, the day before he went, when she asked him whether he wanted rye or French bread for a sandwich, answered in great solemnity – he was becoming interested in the alphabet – 'I'll have a slice of what we people call the F bread.'

She scarcely noticed getting out of the taxi, registering, being conducted to a primitively furnished room. But after she un-

18

packed she remembered Sherrinford had suggested a confidential conference. She went down the hall and knocked on his door. Her knuckles sounded less loud than her heart.

He opened the door, finger on lips, and gestured her toward a corner. Her temper bristled until she saw the image of Chief Constable Dawson in the visiphone. Sherrinford must have chimed him up and must have a reason to keep her out of scanner range. She found a chair and watched, nails digging into knees.

The detective's lean length refolded itself. 'Pardon the interruption,' he said. 'A man mistook the number. Drunk, by the indications.'

Dawson chuckled. 'We get plenty of those.' Barbro recalled his fondness for grabbing. He tugged the beard which he affected, as if he were an outwayer instead of a townsman. 'No harm in them as a rule. They only have a lot of voltage to discharge, after weeks or months in the backlands.'

'I've gathered that that environment – foreign in a million major and minor ways to the one that created man – I've gathered that it does do odd things to the personality.' Sherrinford tamped his pipe. 'Of course, you know my practice has been confined to urban and suburban areas. Isolated garths seldom need private investigators. Now that situation appears to have changed. I called to ask you for advice.'

'Glad to help,' Dawson said. 'I've not forgotten what you did for us in the de Tahoe murder case.' Cautiously: 'Better explain your problem first.'

Sherrinford struck fire. The smoke that followed cut through the green odors – even here, a paved pair of kilometers from the nearest woods – that drifted past traffic rumble through a crepuscular window. 'This is more a scientific mission than a search for an absconding debtor or an industrial spy,' he drawled. 'I'm looking into two possibilities: that an organization, criminal or religious or whatever, has long been active and steals infants; or that the Outlings of folklore are real.'

'Huh?' On Dawson's face Barbro read as much dismay as surprise. 'You can't be serious!'

'Can't I?' Sherrinford smiled. 'Several generations' worth of reports shouldn't be dismissed out of hand. Especially not when they become more frequent and consistent in the course of time, not less. Nor can we ignore the documented loss of babies and small children, amounting by now to over a hundred, and never a trace found afterward. Nor the finds which demonstrate that

19

an intelligent species once inhabited Arctica and may still haunt the interior.'

Dawson leaned forward as if to climb out of the screen. 'Who engaged you?' he demanded. 'That Cullen woman? We were sorry for her, naturally, but she wasn't making sense and when she got downright abusive – '

'Didn't her companions, reputable scientists, confirm her story?'

'No story to confirm. Look, they had the place ringed with detectors and alarms, and they kept mastiffs. Standard procedure in a country where a hungry sauroid or whatever might happen by. Nothing could've entered unbeknownst.'

'On the ground. How about a flyer landing in the middle of camp?'

'A man in a copter rig would've roused everybody.'

'A winged being might be quieter.'

'A living flyer that could lift a three-year-old boy? Doesn't exist.'

'Isn't in the scientific literature, you mean, Constable. Remember Graymantle; remember how little we know about Roland, a planet, an entire world. Such birds do exist on Beowulf – and on Rustum, I've read. I made a calculation from the local ratio of air density to gravity and, yes, it's marginally possible here too. The child could have been carried off for a short distance before wing muscles were exhausted and the creature must descend.'

Dawson snorted. 'First it landed and walked into the tent where mother and boy were asleep. Then it walked away, toting him, after it couldn't fly further. Does that sound like a bird of prey? And the victim didn't cry out, the dogs didn't bark, nothing!'

'As a matter of fact,' Sherrinford said, 'those inconsistencies are the most interesting and convincing feature of the whole account. You're right, it's hard to see how a human kidnapper could get in undetected, and an eagle type of creature wouldn't operate in that fashion. But none of this applies to a winged intelligent being. The boy could have been drugged. Certainly the dogs showed signs of having been.'

'The dogs showed signs of having overslept. Nothing had disturbed them. The kid wandering by wouldn't do so. We don't need to assume one damn thing except, first, that he got restless and, second, that the alarms were a bit sloppily rigged – seeing as how no danger was expected from inside camp – and let him pass out. And, third, I hate to speak this way, but we must assume the poor tyke starved or was killed.'

Dawson paused before adding: 'If we had more staff, we could have given the affair more time. And would have, of course. We did make an aerial sweep, which risked the lives of the pilots, using instruments which would've spotted the kid anywhere in a fifty-kilometer radius, unless he was dead. You know how sensitive thermal analyzers are. We drew a complete blank. We have more important jobs than to hunt for the scattered pieces of a corpse.'

He finished brusquely, 'If Mrs Cullen's hired you, my advice is you find an excuse to quit. Better for her, too. She's got to come to terms with reality.'

Barbro checked a shout by biting her tongue.

'Oh, this is merely the latest disappearance of the series,' Sherrinford said. She didn't understand how he could maintain his easy tone when Jimmy was lost. 'More thoroughly recorded than any before, thus more suggestive. Usually an outwayer family has given a tearful but undetailed account of their child who vanished and must have been stolen by the Old Folk. Sometimes, years later, they'd tell about glimpses of what they swore must have been the grown child, not really human any longer, flitting past in murk or peering through a window or working mischief upon them. As you say, neither the authorities nor the scientists have had personnel or resources to mount a proper investigation. But as I say, the matter appears to be worth investigating. Maybe a private party like myself can contribute.'

'Listen, most of us constables grew up in the outway. We don't just ride patrol and answer emergency calls, we go back there for holidays and reunions. If any gang of . . . of human sacrificers was around, we'd know.'

'I realize that. I also realize that the people you came from have a widespread and deep-seated belief in nonhuman beings with supernatural powers. Many actually go through rites and make offerings to propitiate them.'

'I know what you're leading up to,' Dawson fleered. 'I've heard it before, from a hundred sensationalists. The aborigines are the Outlings. I thought better of you. Surely you've visited a museum or three, surely you've read literature from planets which do have natives – or damn and blast, haven't you ever applied that logic of yours?'

He wagged a finger. 'Think,' he said. 'What have we in fact discovered? A few pieces of worked stone; a few megaliths that might be artificial; scratchings on rock that seem to show plants and animals, though not the way any human culture would ever have shown them; traces of fires and broken bones; other fragments of bone that seem as if they might've belonged to thinking creatures, as if they might've been inside fingers or around big brains. If so, however, the owners looked nothing like men. Or angels, for that matter. Nothing! The most anthropoid reconstruction I've seen shows a kind of two-legged crocagator.

'Wait, let me finish. The stories about the Outlings – oh, I've heard them too, plenty of them; I believed them when I was a kid – the stories tell how there're different kinds, some winged, some not, some half-human, some completely human except maybe for being too handsome – It's fairyland from ancient Earth all over again. Isn't it? I got interested once and dug into the Heritage Library microfiles, and be damned if I didn't find almost the identical yarns, told by peasants centuries before spaceflight.

'None of it squares with the scanty relics we have, if they are relics, or with the fact that no area the size of Arctica could spawn a dozen different intelligent species, or . . . hellfire, man, with the way your common sense tells you aborigines would behave when humans arrived!'

Sherrinford nodded. 'Yes, yes,' he said. 'I'm less sure than you that the common sense of nonhuman beings is precisely like our own. I've seen so much variation within mankind. But, granted, your arguments are strong. Roland's too few scientists have more pressing tasks than tracking down the origins of what is, as you put it, a revived medieval superstition.'

He cradled his pipe bowl in both hands and peered into the tiny hearth of it. 'Perhaps what interests me most,' he said softly, 'is why – across that gap of centuries, across a barrier of machine civilization and its utterly antagonistic world-view – no continuity of tradition whatsoever – why have hardheaded, technologically organized, reasonably well-educated colonists here brought back from its grave a belief in the Old Folk?'

'I suppose eventually, if the University ever does develop the psychology department they keep talking about, I suppose eventually somebody will get a thesis out of that question.' Dawson spoke in a jagged voice, and he gulped when Sherrinford replied:

'I propose to begin now. In Commissioner Hauch Land, since that's where the latest incident occurred. Where can I rent a vehicle?'

'Uh, might be hard to do –'

'Come, come. Tenderfoot or not, I know better. In an economy of scarcity, few people own heavy equipment. But since it's needed, it can always be rented. I want a camper bus with a ground-effect drive suitable for every kind of terrain. And I want certain equipment installed which I've brought along, and the top canopy section replaced by a gun turret controllable from the driver's seat. But I'll supply the weapons. Besides rifles and pistols of my own, I've arranged to borrow some artillery from Christmas Landing's police arsenal.'

'Hoy? Are you genuinely intending to make ready for . . . a war . . . against a myth?'

'Let's say I'm taking out insurance, which isn't terribly expensive, against a remote possibility. Now, besides the bus, what about a light aircraft piggyback for use in surveys?'

'No.' Dawson sounded more positive than hitherto. 'That's asking for disaster. We can have you flown to a base camp in a large plane when the weather report's exactly right. But the pilot will have to fly back at once, before the weather turns wrong again. Meteorology's underdeveloped on Roland, the air's especially treacherous this time of year, and we're not tooled up to produce aircraft that can outlive every surprise.' He drew breath. 'Have you no idea of how fast a whirly-whirly can hit, or what size hailstones might strike from a clear sky, or – ? Once you're there, man, you stick to the ground.' He hesitated. 'That's an important reason our information is so scanty about the outway and its settlers are so isolated.'

Sherrinford laughed ruefully. 'Well, I suppose if details are what I'm after, I must creep along anyway.'

'You'll waste a lot of time,' Dawson said. 'Not to mention your client's money. Listen, I can't forbid you to chase shadows, but – '

The discussion went on for almost an hour. When the screen finally blanked, Sherrinford rose, stretched, and walked toward Barbro. She noticed anew his peculiar gait. He had come from a planet with a fourth again Earth's gravitational drag, to one where weight was less than half Terrestrial. She wondered if he had flying dreams.

'I apologize for shuffling you off like that,' he said. 'I didn't expect to reach him at once. He was quite truthful about how busy he is. But having made contact, I didn't want to remind him overmuch of you. He can dismiss my project as a futile fantasy which I'll soon give up. But he might have frozen completely, might even have put up obstacles before us, if he'd realized through you how determined we are.'

'Why should he care?' she asked in her bitterness.

'Fear of consequences, the worse because it is unadmitted – fear of consequences, the more terrifying because they are unguessable.' Sherrinford's gaze went to the screen, and thence out the window to the aurora pulsing in glacial blue and white immensely far overhead. 'I suppose you saw I was talking to a frightened man. Down underneath his conventionality and scoffing, he believes in the Outlings – oh, yes, he believes.'

The feet of Mistherd flew over yerba and outpaced windblown driftweed. Beside him, black and misshapen, hulked Nagrim the nicor, whose earthquake weight left a swathe of crushed plants. Behind, luminous blossoms of a firethorn shone through the twining, trailing outlines of Morgarel the wraith.

Here Cloudmoor rose in a surf of hills and thickets. The air lay quiet, now and then carrying the distance-muted howl of a beast. It was darker than usual at winterbirth, the moons being down and aurora a wan flicker above mountains on the northern worldedge. But this made the stars keen, and their numbers crowded heaven, and Ghost Road shone among them as if it, like the leafage beneath, were paved with dew.

'Yonder!' bawled Nagrim. All four of his arms pointed. The party had topped a ridge. Far off glimmered a spark. 'Hoah, hoah! 'Ull we right off stamp dem flat, or pluck dem apart slow?'

*We shall do nothing of the sort, bonebrain,* Morgarel's answer slid through their heads. *Not unless they attack us, and they will not unless we make them aware of us, and her command is that we spy out their purposes.*

'Gr-r-rum-m-m. I know deir aim. Cut down trees, stick plows in land, sow deir cursed seed in de clods and in deir shes. 'Less we drive dem into de bitterwater, and soon, soon, dey'll wax too strong for us.'

'Not too strong for the Queen!' Mistherd protested, shocked.

*Yet they do have new powers, it seems,* Morgarel reminded him. *Carefully must we probe them.*

'Den carefully can we step on dem?' asked Nagrim.

The question woke a grin out of Mistherd's own uneasiness. He slapped the scaly back. 'Don't talk, you,' he said 'It hurts my ears. Nor think; that hurts your head. Come, run!'

*Ease yourself,* Morgarel scolded. *You have too much life in you, human-born.*

Mistherd made a face at the wraith, but obeyed to the extent of slowing down and picking his way through what cover the country afforded. For he traveled on behalf of the Fairest, to learn what had brought a pair of mortals questing hither.

Did they seek that boy whom Ayoch stole? (He continued to weep for his mother, though less and less often as the marvels of Carheddin entered him.) Perhaps. A birdcraft had left them and their car at the now abandoned campsite, from which they had followed an outward spiral. But when no trace of the cub had appeared inside a reasonable distance, they did not call to be flown home. And this wasn't because weather forbade the far-speaker waves to travel, as was frequently the case. No, instead the couple set off toward the mountains of Moonhorn. Their course would take them past a few outlying invader steadings and on into realms untrodden by their race.

So this was no ordinary survey. Then what was it?

Mistherd understood now why she who reigned had made her adopted mortal children learn, or retain, the clumsy language of their forebears. He had hated that drill, wholly foreign to Dweller ways. Of course, you obeyed her, and in time you saw how wise she had been . . .

Presently he left Nagrim behind a rock – the nicor would only be useful in a fight – and crawled from bush to bush until he lay within man-lengths of the humans. A rainplant drooped over him, leaves soft on his bare skin, and clothed him in darkness. Morgarel floated to the crown of a shiverleaf, whose unrest would better conceal his flimsy shape. He'd not be much help either. And that was the most troublous, the almost appalling thing here. Wraiths were among those who could not just sense and send thoughts, but cast illusions. Morgarel had reported that this time his power seemed to rebound off an invisible cold wall around the car.

Otherwise the male and female had set up no guardian engines and kept no dogs. Belike they supposed none would be needed, since they slept in the long vehicle which bore them. But such contempt of the Queen's strength could not be tolerated, could it?

Metal sheened faintly by the light of their campfire. They sat on either side, wrapped in coats against a coolness that Mistherd, naked, found mild. The male drank smoke. The female stared past him into a dusk which her flame-dazzled eyes must see as thick gloom. The dancing glow brought her vividly forth. Yes, to judge from Ayoch's tale, she was the dam of the new cub.

Ayoch had wanted to come too, but the Wonderful One forbade. Pooks couldn't hold still long enough for such a mission.

The man sucked on his pipe. His cheeks thus pulled into shadow while the light flickered across nose and brow, he looked disquietingly like a shearbill about to stoop on prey.

' – No, I tell you again, Barbro, I have no theories,' he was saying. 'When facts are insufficient, theorizing is ridiculous at best, misleading at worst.'

'Still, you must have some idea of what you're doing,' she said. It was plain that they had threshed this out often before. No Dweller could be as persistent as her or as patient as him. 'That gear you packed – that generator you keep running – '

'I have a working hypothesis or two, which suggested what equipment I ought to take.'

'Why won't you tell me what the hypotheses are?'

'They themselves indicate that that might be inadvisable at the present time. I'm still feeling my way into the labyrinth. And I haven't had a chance yet to hook everything up. In fact, we're really only protected against so-called telepathic influence – '

'What?' She started. 'Do you mean . . . those legends about how they can read minds too – ' Her words trailed off and her gaze sought the darkness beyond his shoulders.

He leaned forward. His tone lost its clipped rapidity, grew earnest and soft. 'Barbro, you're racking yourself to pieces. Which is no help to Jimmy if he's alive, the more so when you may well be badly needed later on. We've a long trek before us, and you'd better settle into it.'

She nodded jerkily and caught her lip between her teeth for a moment before she answered, 'I'm trying.'

He smiled around his pipe. 'I expect you'll succeed. You don't strike me as a quitter or a whiner or an enjoyer of misery.'

She dropped a hand to the pistol at her belt. Her voice changed; it came out of her throat like knife from sheath. 'When we find them, they'll know what I am. What humans are.'

'Put anger aside also,' the man urged. 'We can't afford emotions. If the Outlings are real, as I told you I'm provisionally assuming, they're fighting for their homes.' After a short stillness he added: 'I like to think that if the first explorers had found live natives, men would not have colonized Roland. But too late now. We can't go back if we wanted to. It's a bitter-end

26

struggle, against an enemy so crafty that he's even hidden from us the fact that he is waging war.'

'Is he? I mean, skulking, kidnapping an occasional child — '

'That's part of my hypothesis. I suspect those aren't harassments, they're tactics employed in a chillingly subtle strategy.'

The fire sputtered and sparked. The man smoked awhile, brooding, until he went on:

'I didn't want to raise your hopes or excite you unduly while you had to wait on me, first in Christmas Landing, then in Portolondon. Afterward we were busy satisfying ourselves Jimmy had been taken further from camp than he could have wandered before collapsing. So I'm only telling you now how thoroughly I studied available material on the . . . Old Folk. Besides, at first I did it on the principle of eliminating every imaginable possibility, however absurd. I expected no result other than final disproof. But I went through everything, relics, analyses, histories, journalistic accounts, monographs; I talked to outwayers who happened to be in town and to what scientists we have who've taken any interest in the matter. I'm a quick study. I flatter myself I became as expert as anyone — though God knows there's little to be expert on. Furthermore, I, a comparative stranger, maybe looked on the problem with fresh eyes. And a pattern emerged for me.

'If the aborigines became extinct, why didn't they leave more remnants? Arctica isn't enormous; and it's fertile for Rolandic life. It ought to have supported a population whose artifacts ought to have accumulated over millennia. I've read that on Earth, literally tens of thousands of paleolithic hand axes were found, more by chance than archaeology.

'Very well. Suppose the relics and fossils were deliberately removed, between the time the last survey party left and the first colonizing ships arrived. I did find some support for that idea in the diaries of the original explorers. They were too preoccupied with checking the habitability of the planet to make catalogues of primitive monuments. However, the remarks they wrote down indicate they saw much more than later arrivals did. Suppose what we have found is just what the removers overlooked or didn't get around to.

'That argues a sophisticated mentality, thinking in long-range terms, doesn't it? Which in turn argues that the Old Folk were not mere hunters or neolithic farmers.'

'But nobody ever saw buildings or machines or any such thing,' Barbro protested.

27

'No. Most likely the natives didn't go through our kind of metallurgic-industrial evolution. I can conceive of other paths to take. Their full-fledged civilization might have begun, rather than ended, in biological science and technology. It might have developed potentialities of the nervous system, which might be greater in their species than in man. We have those abilities to some degree ourselves, you realize. A dowser, for instance, actually senses variations in the local magnetic field caused by a water table. However, in us, these talents are maddeningly rare and tricky. So we took our business elsewhere. Who needs to be a telepath, say, when he has a visiphone? The Old Folk may have seen it the other way around. The artifacts of their civilization may have been, may still be, unrecognizable to men.'

'They could have identified themselves to the men, though,' Barbro said. 'Why didn't they?'

'I can imagine any number of reasons. As, they could have had a bad experience with interstellar visitors earlier in their history. Ours is scarcely the sole race that has spaceships. However, I told you I don't theorize in advance of the facts. Let's say no more than that the Old Folk, if they exist, are alien to us.'

'For a rigorous thinker, you're spinning a mighty thin thread.'

'I've admitted this is entirely provisional.' He squinted at her through a roil of campfire smoke. 'You came to me, Barbro, insisting in the teeth of officialdom your boy had been stolen; but your own talk about cultist kidnappers was ridiculous. Why are you reluctant to admit the reality of nonhumans?'

'In spite of the fact that Jimmy's being alive probably depends on it,' she sighed. 'I know.' A shudder: 'Maybe I don't dare admit it.'

'I've said nothing thus far that hasn't been speculated about in print,' he told her. 'A disreputable speculation, true. In a hundred years, nobody has found valid evidence for the Outlings being more than a superstition. Still, a few people have declared it's at least possible intelligent natives are at large in the wilderness.'

'I know,' she repeated. 'I'm not sure, though, what has made you, overnight, take those arguments seriously.'

'Well, once you got me started thinking, it occurred to me that Roland's outwayers are not utterly isolated medieval crofters. They have books, telecommunications, power tools, motor vehicles, above all they have a modern science-oriented education. Why *should* they turn superstitious? Something must be causing it.' He stopped. 'I'd better not continue. My ideas

28

go further than this; but if they're correct, it's dangerous to speak them aloud.'

Mistherd's belly muscles tensed. There was danger for fair, in that shearbill head. The Garland Bearer must be warned. For a minute he wondered about summoning Nagrim to kill these two. If the nicor jumped them fast, their firearms might avail them naught. But no. They might have left word at home, or —
He came back to his ears. The talk had changed course. Barbro was murmuring, ' — why you stayed on Roland.'

The man smiled his gaunt smile. 'Well, life on Beowulf held no challenge for me. Heorot is — or was; this was decades past, remember — Heorot was densely populated, smoothly organized, boringly uniform. That was partly due to the lowland frontier, a safety valve that bled off the dissatisfied. But I lack the carbon-dioxide tolerance necessary to live healthily down there. An expedition was being readied to make a swing around a number of colony worlds, especially those which didn't have the equipment to keep in laser contact. You'll recall its announced purpose, to seek out new ideas in science, arts, sociology, philosophy, whatever might prove valuable. I'm afraid they found little on Roland relevant to Beowolf. But I, who had wangled a berth, I saw opportunities for myself and decided to make my home here.'

'Were you a detective back there, too?'

'Yes, in the official police. We had a tradition of such work in our family. Some of that may have come from the Cherokee side of it, if the name means anything to you. However, we also claimed collateral descent from one of the first private inquiry agents on record, back on Earth before spaceflight. Regardless of how true that may be, I found him a useful model. You see, an archetype — '

The man broke off. Unease crossed his features. 'Best we go to sleep,' he said. 'We've a long distance to cover in the morning.'

She looked outward. 'Here is no morning.'

They retired. Mistherd rose and cautiously flexed limberness back into his muscles. Before returning to the Sister of Lyrth, he risked a glance through a pane in the car. Bunks were made up, side by side, and the humans lay in them. Yet the man had not touched her, though hers was a bonny body, and nothing that had passed between them suggested he meant to do so.

Eldritch, humans. Cold and claylike. And they would over-run the beautiful wild world? Mistherd spat in disgust. It must

29

not happen. It would not happen. She who reigned had vowed that.

The lands of William Irons were immense. But this was because a barony was required to support him, his kin and cattle, on native crops whose cultivation was still poorly understood. He raised some Terrestrial plants as well, by summerlight and in conservatories. However, these were a luxury. The true conquest of northern Arctica lay in yerba hay, in bathyrhiza wood, in pericoup and glycophyllon and eventually, when the market had expanded with population and industry, in chalcanthemum for city florists and pelts of cage-bred rover for city furriers.

That was in a tomorrow Irons did not expect he would live to see. Sherrinford wondered if the man really expected anyone ever would.

The room was warm and bright. Cheerfulness crackled in the fireplace. Light from fluoropanels gleamed off hand-carven chests and chairs and tables, off colorful draperies and shelved dishes. The outwayer sat solid in his highseat, stoutly clad, beard flowing down his chest. His wife and daughters brought coffee, whose fragrance joined the remnant odors of a hearty supper, to him, his guests, and his sons.

But outside, wind hooted, lightning flared, thunder bawled, rain crashed on roof and walls and roared down to swirl among the courtyard cobblestones. Sheds and barns crouched against hugeness beyond. Trees groaned; and did a wicked undertone of laughter run beneath the lowing of a frightened cow? A burst of hailstones hit the tiles like knocking knuckles.

You could feel how distant your neighbors were, Sherrinford thought. And nonetheless they were the people whom you saw oftenest, did daily business with by visiphone (when a solar storm didn't make gibberish of their voices and chaos of their faces) or in the flesh, partied with, gossipped and intrigued with, intermarried with; in the end, they were the people who would bury you. The lights and machinery of the coastal towns were monstrously farther away.

William Irons was a strong man. Yet when now he spoke, fear was in his tone. 'You'd truly go over Troll Scarp?'

'Do you mean Hanstein Palisades?' Sherrinford responded, more challenge than question.

'No outwayer calls it anything but Troll Scarp,' Barbro said.

And how had a name like that been reborn, light-years and centuries from Earth's dark ages?

'Hunters, trappers, prospectors – rangers, you call them – travel in those mountains,' Sherrinford declared.

'In certain parts,' Irons said. 'That's allowed, by a pact once made 'tween a man and the Queen after he'd done well by a jack-o'-the-hill that a satan had hurt. Wherever the plumablanca grows, men may fare, if they leave mangoods on the altar boulders in payment for what they take out of the land. Elsewhere – ' one fist clenched on a chair arm and went slack again – ' 's not wise to go.'

'It's been done, hasn't it?'

'Oh, yes. And some came back all right, or so they claimed, though I've heard they were never lucky afterward. And some didn't, they vanished. And some who returned babbled of wonders and horrors, and stayed witlings the rest of their lives. Not for a long time has anybody been rash enough to break the pact and overtread the bounds.' Irons looked at Barbro almost entreatingly. His woman and children stared likewise, grown still. Wind hooted beyond the walls and rattled the storm shutters. 'Don't you.'

'I've reason to believe my son is there,' she answered.

'Yes, yes, you've told and I'm sorry. Maybe something can be done. I don't know what, but I'd be glad to, oh, lay a double offering on Unvar's Barrow this midwinter, and a prayer drawn in the turf by a flint knife. Maybe they'll return him.' Irons sighed. 'They've not done such a thing in man's memory, though. And he could have a worse lot. I've glimpsed them myself, speeding madcap through twilight. They seem happier than we are. Might be no kindness, sending your boy home again.'

'Like in the Arvid song,' said his wife.

Irons nodded. 'M-hm. Or others, come to think of it.'

'What's this?' Sherrinford asked. More sharply than before, he felt himself a stranger. He was a child of cities and technics, above all a child of the skeptical intelligence. This family *believed*. It was disquieting to see more than a touch of their acceptance in Barbro's slow nod.

'We have the same ballad in Olga Ivanoff Land,' she told him, her voice less calm than the words. 'It's one of the traditional ones, nobody knows who composed them, that are sung to set the measure of a ring-dance in a meadow.'

'I noticed a multilyre in your baggage, Mrs Cullen,' said the wife of Irons. She was obviously eager to get off the explosive topic of a venture in defiance of the Old Folk. A songfest could help. 'Would you like to entertain us?'

31

Barbro shook her head, white around the nostrils. The oldest boy said quickly, rather importantly, 'Well, sure, I can, if our guests would like to hear.'

'I'd enjoy that, thank you.' Sherrinford leaned back in his seat and stroked his pipe. If this had not happened spontaneously, he would have guided the conversation toward a similar outcome.

In the past he had had no incentive to study the folklore of the outway, and not much chance to read the scanty references on it since Barbro brought him her trouble. Yet more and more he was becoming convinced he must get an understanding – not an anthropological study; a feel from the inside out – of the relationship between Roland's frontiersmen and those beings which haunted them.

A bustling followed, rearrangement, settling down to listen, coffee cups refilled and brandy offered on the side. The boy explained, 'The last line is the chorus. Everybody join in, right?' Clearly he too hoped thus to bleed off some of the tension. Catharsis through music? Sherrinford wondered, and added to himself: No; exorcism.

A girl strummed a guitar. The boy sang, to a melody which beat across the storm-noise:

'It was the ranger Arvid
rode homeward through the hills
among the shadowy shiverleafs,
along the chiming hills.
*The dance weaves under the firethorn.*


'The night wind whispered around him
with scent of brok and rue.
Both moons rose high above him
and hills aflash with dew.
*The dance weaves under the firethorn.*


'And dreaming of that woman
who waited in the sun,
he stopped, amazed by starlight,
and so he was undone.
*The dance weaves under the firethorn.*


'For there beneath a barrow
that bulked athwart a moon,
the Outling folk were dancing

32

in glass and golden shoon.
*The dance weaves under the firethorn.*

'The Outling folk were dancing
like water, wind and fire
to frosty-ringing harpstrings,
and never did they tire.
*The dance weaves under the firethorn.*

'To Arvid came she striding
from where she watched the dance,
the Queen of Air and Darkness,
with starlight in her glance.
*The dance weaves under the firethorn.*

'With starlight, love, and terror
in her immortal eye,
the Queen of Air and Darkness – '

'No!' Barbro leaped from her chair. Her fists were clenched
and tears flogged her cheekbones. 'You can't – pretend that –
about the things that stole Jimmy!'

She fled from the chamber, upstairs to her guest bedroom.

But she finished the song herself. That was about seventy hours
later, camped in the steeps where rangers dared not fare.

She and Sherrinford had not said much to the Irons family
after refusing repeated pleas to leave the forbidden country
alone. Nor had they exchanged many remarks at first as they
drove north. Slowly, however, he began to draw her out about
her own life. After a while she almost forgot to mourn, in her
remembering of home and old neighbors. Somehow this led to
discoveries – that he beneath his professional manner was a
gourmet and a lover of opera and appreciated her femaleness;
that she could still laugh and find beauty in the wild land
around her – and she realized, half guiltily, that life held more
hopes than even the recovery of the son Tim gave her.

'I've convinced myself he's alive,' the detective said. He
scowled. 'Frankly, it makes me regret having taken you along. I
expected this would be only a fact-gathering trip, but it's turning out to be more. If we're dealing with real creatures who
stole him, they can do real harm. I ought to turn back to the
nearest garth and call for a plane to fetch you.'

'Like bottommost hell you will, mister,' she said. 'You need somebody who knows outway conditions; and I'm a better shot than average.'

'M-m-m . . . it would involve considerable delay too, wouldn't it? Besides the added distance, I can't put a signal through to any airport before this current burst of solar interference has calmed down.'

Next 'night' he broke out his remaining equipment and set it up. She recognized some of it, such as the thermal detector. Other items were strange to her, copied to his order from the advanced apparatus of his birthworld. He would tell her little about them. 'I've explained my suspicion that the ones we're after have telepathic capabilities,' he said in apology.

Her eyes widened. 'You mean it could be true, the Queen and her people can read minds?'

'That's part of the dread which surrounds their legend, isn't it? Actually there's nothing spooky about the phenomenon. It was studied and fairly well defined centuries ago, on Earth. I daresay the facts are available in the scientific microfiles and Christmas Landing. You Rolanders have simply had no occasion to seek them out, any more than you've yet had occasion to look up how to build power beamcasters or spacecraft.'

'Well, how does telepathy work, then?'

Sherrinford recognized that her query asked for comfort as much as it did for facts, and spoke with deliberate dryness: 'The organism generates extremely long-wave radiation which can, in principle, be modulated by the nervous system. In practice, the feebleness of the signals and their low rate of information transmission make them elusive, hard to detect and measure. Our prehuman ancestors went in for more reliable senses, like vision and hearing. What telepathic transceiving we do is marginal at best. But explorers have found extraterrestrial species that got an evolutionary advantage from developing the system further, in their particular environments. I imagine such species could include one which gets comparatively little direct sunlight – in fact, appears to hide from broad day. It could even become so able in this regard that, at short range, it can pick up man's weak emissions and make man's primitive sensitivities resonate to its own strong sendings.'

'That would account for a lot, wouldn't it?' Barbro asked faintly.

'I've now screened our car by a jamming field,' Sherrinford told her, 'but it reaches only a few metres past the chassis.

Beyond, a scout of theirs might get a warning from your thoughts, if you knew precisely what I'm trying to do. I have a well-trained subconscious which sees to it that I think about this in French when I'm outside. Communication has to be structured to be intelligible, you see, and that's a different enough structure from English. But English is the only human language on Roland, and surely the Old Folk have learned it.'

She nodded. He had told her his general plan, which was too obvious to conceal. The problem was to make contact with the aliens, if they existed. Hitherto they had only revealed themselves, at rare intervals, to one or a few backwoodsmen at a time. An ability to generate hallucinations would help them in that. They would stay clear of any large, perhaps unmanageable expedition which might pass through their territory. But two people, braving all prohibitions, shouldn't look too formidable to approach. And . . . this would be the first human team which not only worked on the assumption that the Outlings were real but possessed the resources of modern, off-planet police technology.

Nothing happened at that camp. Sherrinford said he hadn't expected it would. The Old Folk seemed cautious this near to any settlement. In their own lands they must be bolder.

And by the following 'night', the vehicle had gone well into yonder country. When Sherrinford stopped the engine in a meadow and the car settled down, silence rolled in like a wave.

They stepped out. She cooked a meal on the glower while he gathered wood, that they might later cheer themselves with a campfire. Frequently he glanced at his wrist. It bore no watch – instead, a radio-controlled dial, to tell what the instruments in the bus might register.

Who needed a watch here? Slow constellations wheeled beyond glimmering aurora. The moon Alde stood above a snow-peak, turning it argent, though this place lay at a goodly height. The rest of the mountains were hidden by the forest that crowded around. Its trees were mostly shiverleaf and feathery white plumablanca, ghostly amid their shadows. A few fire-thorns glowed, clustered dim lanterns, and the underbrush was heavy and smelled sweet. You could see surprisingly far through the blue dusk. Somewhere nearby a brook sang and a bird fluted.

'Lovely here,' Sherrinford said. They had risen from their supper and not yet sat down or kindled their fire.

'But strange,' Barbro answered as low. 'I wonder if it's really meant for us. If we can really hope to possess it.'

His pipestem gestured at the stars. 'Man's gone to stranger places than this.'

'Has he? I . . . oh, I suppose it's just something left over from my outway childhood, but do you know, when I'm under them I can't think of the stars as balls of gas, whose energies have been measured, whose planets have been walked on by prosaic feet. No, they're small and cold and magical; our lives are bound to them; after we die, they whisper to us in our graves.' Barbro glanced downward. 'I realize that's nonsense.'

She could see in the twilight how his face grew tight. 'Not at all,' he said. 'Emotionally, physics may be a worse nonsense. And in the end, you know, after a sufficient number of generations, thought follows feeling. Man is not at heart rational. He could stop believing the stories of science if those no longer felt right.'

He paused. 'That ballad which didn't get finished in the house,' he said, not looking at her. 'Why did it affect you so?'

'I was overwrought. I couldn't stand hearing *them,* well, praised. Or that's how it seemed. My apologies for the fuss.'

'I gather the ballad is typical of a large class.'

'Well, I never thought to add them up. Cultural anthropology is something we don't have time for on Roland, or more likely it hasn't occurred to us, with everything else there is to do. But – now you mention it, yes, I'm surprised at how many songs and stories have the Arvid motif in them.'

'Could you bear to recite it for me?'

She mustered the will to laugh. 'Why, I can do better than that if you want. Let me get my multilyre and I'll perform.'

She omitted the hypnotic chorus line, though, when the notes rang out, except at the end. He watched her where she stood against moon and aurora.

' – the Queen of Air and Darkness
cried softly under sky:

' "Light down, you ranger Arvid,
and join the Outling folk.
You need no more be human,
which is a heavy yoke."

'He dared to give her answer:
"I may do naught but run.
A maiden waits me, dreaming
in lands beneath the sun.

' "And likewise wait me comrades
and tasks I would not shirk,
for what is Ranger Arvid
if he lays down his work?

' "So wreak your spells, you Outling,
and cast your wrath on me.
Though maybe you can slay me,
you'll not make me unfree."

'The Queen of Air and Darkness
stood wrapped about with fear
and northlight-flares and beauty
he dared not look too near.

'Until she laughed like harpsong
and said to him in scorn:
"I do not need a magic
to make you always mourn.

' "I send you home with nothing
except your memory
of moonlight, Outling music,
night breezes, dew, and me.

' "And that will run behind you,
a shadow on the sun,
and that will lie beside you
when every day is done.

' "In work and play and friendship
your grief will strike you dumb
for thinking what you are – and –
what you might have become.

' "Your dull and foolish woman
treat kindly as you can.
Go home now, Ranger Arvid,
set free to be a man!"

'In flickering and laughter
the Outling folk were gone.
He stood alone by moonlight
and wept until the dawn.
     *The dance weaves under the firethorn.*'

She laid the lyre aside. A wind rustled leaves. After a long quietness Sherrinford said, 'And tales of this kind are part of everyone's life in the outway?'

'Well, you could put it thus,' Barbro replied. 'Though they're not all full of supernatural doings. Some are about love or heroism. Traditional themes.'

'I don't think your particular tradition has arisen of itself.' His tone was bleak. 'In fact, I think many of your songs and stories were not composed by humans.'

He snapped his lips shut and would say no more on the subject. They went early to bed.

Hours later, an alarm roused them.

The buzzing was soft, but it brought them instantly alert. They slept in gripsuits, to be prepared for emergencies. Sky-glow lit them through the canopy. Sherrinford swung out of his bunk, slipped shoes on feet and clipped gun holster to belt. 'Stay inside,' he commanded.

'What's here?' Her pulse thudded.

He squinted at the dials of his instruments and checked them against the luminous telltale on his wrist. 'Three animals,' he counted. 'Not wild ones happening by. A large one, homeothermic, to judge from the infrared, holding still a short ways off. Another . . . hm, low temperature, diffuse and unstable emission, as if it were more like a . . . a swarm of cells coordinated somehow . . . pheromonally? . . . hovering, also at a distance. But the third's practically next to us, moving around in the brush; and that pattern looks human.'

She saw him quiver with eagerness, no longer seeming a professor. 'I'm going to try to make a capture,' he said. 'When we have a subject for interrogation – Stand ready to let me back in again fast. But don't risk yourself, whatever happens. And keep this cocked.' He handed her a loaded big-game rifle.

His tall frame poised by the door, opened it a crack. Air blew in, cool, damp, full of fragrances and murmurings. The moon Oliver was now also aloft, the radiance of both unreally brilliant, and the aurora seethed in whiteness and ice-blue.

Sherrinford peered afresh at his telltale. It must indicate the directions of the watchers, among those dappled leaves. Abruptly he sprang out. He sprinted past the ashes of the campfire and vanished under trees. Barbro's hand strained on the butt of her weapon.

Racket exploded. Two in combat burst onto the meadow. Sherrinford had clapped a grip on a smaller human figure. She could make out by streaming silver and rainbow flicker that the other was nude, male, long-haired, lithe, and young. He fought demoniacally, seeking to use teeth and feet and raking nails, and meanwhile he ululated like a satan.

The identification shot through her: A changeling, stolen in babyhood and raised by the Old Folk. This creature was what they would make Jimmy into.

'Ha!' Sherrinford forced his opponent around and drove stiffened fingers into the solar plexus. The boy gasped and sagged. Sherrinford manhandled him toward the car.

Out from the woods came a giant. It might itself have been a tree, black and rugose, bearing four great gnarly boughs; but earth quivered and boomed beneath its leg-roots, and its hoarse bellowing filled sky and skulls.

Barbro shrieked. Sherrinford whirled. He yanked out his pistol, fired and fired, flat whipcracks through the half-light. His free arm kept a lock on the youth. The troll shape lurched under those blows. It recovered and came on, more slowly, more carefully, circling around to cut him off from the bus. He couldn't move fast enough to evade unless he released his prisoner – who was his sole possible guide to Jimmy –

Barbro leaped forth. 'Don't!' Sherrinford shouted. 'For God's sake, stay inside!' The monster rumbled and made snatching motions at her. She pulled trigger. Recoil slammed her in the shoulder. The colossus rocked and fell. Somehow it got its feet back and lumbered toward her. She retreated. Again she shot and again. The creature snarled. Blood began to drip from it and gleam oilily amidst dewdrops. It turned and went off, breaking branches, into the darkness that laired beneath the woods.

'Get to shelter!' Sherrinford yelled. 'You're out of the jammer field!'

A mistiness drifted by overhead. She barely glimpsed it before she saw the new shape at the meadow edge. 'Jimmy!' tore from her.

'Mother.' He held out his arms. Moonlight coursed in his tears. She dropped her weapon and ran to him.

Sherrinford plunged in pursuit. Jimmy flitted away into the brush. Barbro crashed after, through clawing twigs. Then she was seized and borne away.

Standing over his captive, Sherrinford strengthened the fluoro output until vision of the wilderness was blocked off from within the bus. The boy squirmed beneath that colorless glare.

'You are going to talk,' the man said. Despite the haggardness in his features, he spoke quietly.

The boy glowered through tangled locks. A bruise was purpling on his jaw. He'd almost recovered ability to flee while Sherrinford chased and lost the woman. Returning, the detective had barely caught him. Time was lacking to be gentle, when Outling reinforcements might arrive at any moment. Sherrinford had knocked him out and dragged him inside. Now he sat lashed into a swivel seat.

He spat. 'Talk to you, man-clod?' But sweat stood on his skin and his eyes flickered unceasingly around the metal which caged him.

'Give me a name to call you by.'

'And have you work a spell on me?'

'Mine's Eric. If you don't give me another choice, I'll have to call you . . . m-m-m . . . Wuddikins.'

'What?' However eldritch, the bound one remained a human adolescent. 'Mistherd, then.' The lilting accent of his English somehow emphasized its sullenness. 'That's not the sound, only what it means. Anyway, it's my spoken name, naught else.'

'Ah, you keep a secret name you consider to be real?'

'She does. I don't know myself what it is. She knows the real names of everybody.'

Sherrinford raised his brows. 'She?'

'Who reigns. May she forgive me, I can't make the reverent sign when my arms are tied. Some invaders call her the Queen of Air and Darkness.'

'So.' Sherrinford got pipe and tobacco. He let silence wax while he started the fire. At length he said:

'I'll confess the Old Folk took me by surprise. I didn't expect so formidable a member of your gang. Everything I could learn had seemed to show they work on my race – and yours, lad – by stealth, trickery, and illusion.'

Mistherd jerked a truculent nod. 'She created the first nicors not long ago. Don't think she has naught but dazzlements at her beck.'

'I don't. However, a steel-jacketed bullet works pretty well too, doesn't it?'

Sherrinford talked on, softly, mostly to himself: 'I do still believe the, ah, nicors – all your half-humanlike breeds – are intended in the main to be seen, not used. The power of projecting mirages must surely be quite limited in range and scope as well as in the number of individuals who possess it. Otherwise

40

she wouldn't have needed to work as slowly and craftily as she has. Even outside our mind-shield, Barbro – my companion – could have resisted, could have remained aware that whatever she saw was unreal . . . if she'd been less shaken, less frantic, less driven by need.'

Sherrinford wreathed his head in smoke. 'Never mind what I experienced,' he said. 'It couldn't have been the same as for her. I think the command was simply given us, "You will see what you most desire in the world, running away from you into the forest." Of course, she didn't travel many meters before the nicor waylaid her. I'd no hope of trailing them; I'm no Arctican woodsman, and besides, it'd have been too easy to ambush me. I came back to you.' Grimly: 'You're my link to your overlady.'

'You think I'll guide you to Starhaven or Carheddin? Try making me, clod-man.'

'I want to bargain.'

'I s'pect you intend more'n that.' Mistherd's answer held surprising shrewdness. 'What'll you tell after you come home?'

'Yes, that does pose a problem, doesn't it? Barbro Cullen and I are not terrified outwayers. We're of the city. We brought recording instruments. We'd be the first of our kind to report an encounter with the Old Folk, and that report would be detailed and plausible. It would produce action.'

'So you see I'm not afraid to die,' Mistheard declared, though his lips trembled a bit. 'If I let you come in and do your manthings to my people, I'd have naught left living for.'

'Have no immediate fears,' Sherrinford said. 'You're merely bait.' He sat down and regarded the boy through a visor of calm. (Within, it wept in him: *Barbro, Barbro!*) 'Consider. Your Queen can't very well let me go back, bringing my prisoner and telling about hers. She has to stop that somehow. I could try fighting my way through – this car is better armed than you know – but that wouldn't free anybody. Instead, I'm staying put. New forces of hers will get here as fast as they can. I assume they won't blindly throw themselves against a machine gun, a howitzer, a fulgurator. They'll parley first, whether their intentions are honest or not. Thus I make the contact I'm after.'

'What d'you plan?' The mumble held anguish.

'First, this, as a sort of invitation.' Sherrinford reached out to flick a switch. 'There. I've lowered my shield against mind-reading and shape-casting. I daresay the leaders, as least, will be able to sense that it's gone. That should give them confidence.'

'And next?'

'Why, next we wait. Would you like something to eat or drink?'

During the time which followed, Sherrinford tried to jolly Mistherd along, find out something of his life. What answers he got were curt. He dimmed the interior lights and settled down to peer outward. That was a long few hours.

They ended at a shout of gladness, half a sob, from the boy. Out of the woods came a band of the Old Folk.

Some of them stood forth more clearly than moons and stars and northlights should have caused. He in the van rode a white crownbuck whose horns were garlanded. His form was manlike but unearthly beautiful, silver-blond hair falling from beneath the antlered helmet, around the proud cold face. The cloak fluttered off his back like living wings. His frost-colored mail rang as he fared.

Behind him, to right and left, rode two who bore swords whereon small flames gleamed and flickered. Above, a flying flock laughed and trilled and tumbled in the breeze. Near them drifted a half-transparent mistiness. Those others who passed among trees after their chieftain were harder to make out. But they moved in quicksilver grace, and as it were to a sound of harps and trumpets.

'Lord Luighaid.' Glory overflowed in Mistherd's tone. 'Her master Knower – himself.'

Sherrinford had never done a harder thing than to sit at the main control panel, finger near the button of the shield generator, and not touch it. He rolled down a section of canopy to let voices travel. A gust of wind struck him in the face, bearing odors of the roses in his mother's garden. At his back, in the main body of the vehicle, Mistherd strained against his bonds till he could see the incoming troop.

'Call to them,' Sherrinford said. 'Ask if they will talk with me.'

Unknown, flutingly sweet words flew back and forth. 'Yes,' the boy interpreted. 'He will, the Lord Luighaid. But I can tell you, you'll never be let go. Don't fight them. Yield. Come away. You don't know what 'tis to be alive till you've dwelt in Carheddin under the mountain.'

The Outlings drew nigh.

Jimmy glimmered and was gone. Barbro lay in strong arms against a broad breast, and felt the horse move beneath her. It had to be a horse, though only a few were kept any longer on the steadings, and they for special uses or love. She could feel the rippling beneath its hide, hear a rush of parted leafage and the thud when a hoof struck stone; warmth and living scent welled up around her through the darkness.

He who carried her said mildly, 'Don't be afraid, darling. It was a vision. But he's waiting for us and we're bound for him.'

She was aware in a vague way that she ought to feel terror or despair or something. But her memories lay behind her – she wasn't sure just how she had come to be here – she was borne along in a knowledge of being loved. At peace, at peace, rest in the calm expectation of joy . . .

After a while the forest opened. They crossed a lea where boulders stood gray-white under the moons, their shadows shifting in the dim hues which the aurora threw across them. Flitteries danced, tiny comets, above the flowers between. Ahead gleamed a peak whose top was crowned in clouds.

Barbro's eyes happened to be turned forward. She saw the horse's head and thought, with quiet surprise: Why, this is Sambo, who was mine when I was a girl. She looked upward at the man. He wore a black tunic and a cowled cape, which made his face hard to see. She could not cry aloud, here. 'Tim,' she whispered.

'Yes, Barbro.'

'I buried you – '

His smile was endlessly tender. 'Did you think we're no more than what's laid back into the ground? Poor torn sweetheart. She who's called us is the All Healer. Now rest and dream.'

'Dream,' she said, and for a space she struggled to rouse herself. But the effort was weak. Why should she believe ashen tales about . . . atoms and energies, nothing else to fill a gape of emptiness . . . tales she could not bring to mind . . . when Tim and the horse her father gave her carried her on to Jimmy? Had the other thing not been the evil dream, and this her first drowsy awakening from it?

As if he heard her thoughts, he murmured, 'They have a song in Outling lands. The Song of the Men:

'The world sails
to an unseen wind.
Light swirls by the bows.
The wake is night.
But the Dwellers have no such sadness.'

43

'I don't understand,' she said.

He nodded. 'There's much you'll have to understand, darling, and I can't see you again until you've learned those truths. But meanwhile you'll be with our son.'

She tried to lift her head and kiss him. He held her down. 'Not yet,' he said. 'You've not been received among the Queen's people. I shouldn't have come for you, except that she was too merciful to forbid. Lie back, lie back.'

Time blew past. The horse galloped tireless, never stumbling, up the mountain. Once she glimpsed a troop riding down it and thought they were bound for a last weird battle in the west against . . . who? . . . one who lay cased in iron and sorrow – Later she would ask herself the name of him who had brought her into the land of the Old Truth.

Finally spires lifted splendid among the stars, which are small and magical and whose whisperings comfort us after we are dead. They rode into a courtyard where candles burned unwavering, fountains splashed and birds sang. The air bore fragrance of brok and pericoup, of rue and roses; for not everything that man brought was horrible. The Dwellers waited in beauty to welcome her. Beyond their stateliness, pooks cavorted through the gloaming; among the trees darted children; merriment caroled across music more solemn.

'We have come – ' Tim's voice was suddenly, inexplicably a croak. Barbro was not sure how he dismounted, bearing her. She stood before him and saw him sway on his feet.

Fear caught her. 'Are you well?' She seized both his hands. They felt cold and rough. Where had Sambo gone? Her eyes searched beneath the cowl. In this brighter illumination, she ought to have seen her man's face clearly. But it was blurred, it kept changing. 'What's wrong, oh, what's happened?'

He smiled. Was that the smile she had cherished? She couldn't completely remember. 'I, I must go,' he stammered, so low she could scarcely hear. 'Our time is not ready.' He drew free of her grasp and leaned on a robed form which had appeared at his side. A haziness swirled over both their heads. 'Don't watch me go . . . back into the earth,' he pleaded. 'That's death for you. Till our time returns – There, our son!'

She had to fling her gaze around. Kneeling, she spread wide her arms. Jimmy struck her like a warm, solid cannonball. She rumpled his hair, she kissed the hollow of his neck, she laughed and wept and babbled foolishness; and this was no ghost, no memory that had stolen off when she wasn't looking. Now and again, as she turned her attention to yet another hurt which might have come upon him – hunger, sickness, fear – and found none, she would glimpse their surroundings. The gardens were gone. It didn't matter.

'I misted you so, Mother. Stay?'

'I'll take you home, dearest.'

'Stay. Here's fun. I'll show. But you stay.'

A sighing went through the twilight. Barbro rose. Jimmy clung to her hand. They confronted the Queen.

Very tall she was in her robes woven of northlights, and her starry crown and her garlands of kiss-me-never. Her countenance recalled Aphrodite of Milos, whose picture Barbro had often seen in the realms of men, save that the Queen's was more fair, and more majesty dwelt upon it and in the night-blue eyes. Around her the gardens woke to new reality, the court of the Dwellers and the heaven-climbing spires.

'Be welcome,' she spoke, her speaking a song, 'forever.'

Against the awe of her, Barbro said, 'Moonmother, let us go home.'

'That may not be.'

'To our world, little and beloved,' Barbro dreamed she begged, 'which we build for ourselves and cherish for our children.'

'To prison days, angry nights, works that crumble in the fingers, loves that turn to rot or stone or driftweed, loss, grief, and the only sureness that of the final nothingness. No. You too, Wanderfoot who is to be, will jubilate when the banners of the Outworld come flying into the last of the cities and man is made wholly alive. Now go with those who will teach you.'

The Queen of Air and Darkness lifted an arm in summons. It halted, and none came to answer.

For over the fountains and melodies lifted a gruesome growling. Fires leaped, thunders crashed. Her hosts scattered screaming before the steel thing which boomed up the mountainside. The pooks were gone in a whirl of frightened wings. The nicors flung their bodies against the unalive invader and were consumed, until their Mother cried to them to retreat.

Barbro cast Jimmy down and herself over him. Towers wavered and smoked away. The mountain stood bare under icy moons, save for rocks, crags, and further off a glacier in whose depths the auroral light pulsed blue. A cave mouth darkened a cliff. Thither folk streamed, seeking refuge underground. Some were human of blood, some grotesques like the pooks and nicors

45

and wraiths; but most were lean, scaly, long-tailed, long-beaked, not remotely men or Outlings.

For an instant, even as Jimmy wailed at her breast – perhaps as much because the enchantment had been wrecked as because he was afraid – Barbro pitied the Queen who stood alone in her nakedness. Then that one also had fled, and Barbro's world shivered apart.

The guns fell silent, the vehicle whirred to a halt. From it sprang a boy who called wildly, 'Shadow-of-a-Dream, where are you? It's me, Mistherd, oh, come, come!' – before he remembered that the language they had been raised in was not man's. He shouted in that until a girl crept out of a thicket where she had hidden. They stared at each other through dust, smoke, and moonglow. She ran to him.

A new voice barked from the car, 'Barbro, hurry!'

Christmas Landing knew day: short at this time of year, but sunlight, blue skies, white clouds, glittering water, salt breezes in busy streets, and the sane disorder of Eric Sherrinford's living-room.

He crossed and uncrossed his legs where he sat, puffed on his pipe as if to make a veil, and said, 'Are you certain you're recovered? You mustn't risk overstrain.'

'I'm fine,' Barbro Cullen replied, though her tone was flat. 'Still tired, yes, and showing it, no doubt. One doesn't go through such an experience and bounce back in a week. But I'm up and about. And to be frank, I must know what's happened, what's going on, before I can settle down to regain my full strength. Not a word of news anywhere.'

'Have you spoken to others about the matter?'

'No. I've simply told visitors I was too exhausted to talk. Not much of a lie. I assumed there's a reason for censorship.'

Sherrinford looked relieved. 'Good girl. It's at my urging. You can imagine the sensation when this is made public. The authorities agreed they need time to study the facts, think and debate in a calm atmosphere, have a decent policy ready to offer voters who're bound to become rather hysterical at first.' His mouth quirked slightly upward. 'Furthermore, your nerves and Jimmy's get their chance to heal before the journalistic storm breaks over you. How is he?'

'Quite well. He continues pestering me for leave to go play with his friends in the Wonderful Place. But at his age, he'll recover – he'll forget.'

46

'He may meet them later anyhow.'

'What? We didn't — ' Barbro shifted in her chair. 'I've forgotten too. I hardly recall a thing from our last hours. Did you bring back any kidnapped humans?'

'No. The shock was savage, as was, without throwing them straight into an . . . an institution. Mistherd, who's basically a sensible young fellow, assured me they'd get along, at any rate as regards survival necessities, till arrangements can be made.' Sherrinford hesitated. 'I'm not sure what the arrangements will be. Nobody is, at our present stage. But obviously they include those people — or many of them, especially those who aren't full-grown — rejoining the human race. Though they may never feel at home in civilization. Perhaps in a way that's best,· since we will need some kind of mutually acceptable liaison with the Dwellers.'

His impersonality soothed them both. Barbro became able to say, 'Was I too big a fool? I do remember how I yowled and beat my head on the floor.'

'Why, no.' He considered the big woman and her pride for a few seconds before he rose, walked over and laid a hand on her shoulder. 'You'd been lured and trapped by a skillful play on your deepest instincts, at a moment of sheer nightmare. Afterward, as that wounded monster carried you off, evidently another type of being came along, one that could saturate you with close-range neuropsychic forces. On top of this, my arrival, the sudden brutal abolishment of every hallucination, must have been shattering. No wonder if you cried out in pain. Before you did, you completely got Jimmy and yourself into the bus, and you never interfered with me.'

'What did you do?'

'Why, I drove off as fast as possible. After several hours, the atmospherics let up sufficiently for me to call Portolondon and insist on an emergency airlift. Not that that was vital. What chance has the enemy to stop us? They didn't even try. But quick transportation was certainly helpful.'

'I figured that's what must have gone on.' Barbro caught his glance. 'No, what I meant was, how did you find us in the backlands?'

Sherrinford moved a little off from her. 'My prisoner was my guide. I don't think I actually killed any of the Dwellers who'd come to deal with me. I hope not. The car simply broke through them, after a couple of warning shots, and afterward outpaced them. Steel and fuel against flesh wasn't really fair. At the cave

47

entrance, I did have to shoot down a few of those troll creatures. I'm not proud of it.'

He stood silent. Presently: 'But you were a captive,' he said. 'I couldn't be sure what they might do to you, who had first claim on me.' After another pause: 'I don't look for any more violence.'

'How did you make . . . the boy . . . cooperate?'

Sherrinford paced from her, to the window, where he stood staring out at the Boreal Ocean. 'I turned off the mind shield,' he said. 'I let their band get close, in full splendor of illusion. Then I turned the shield back on and we both saw them in their true shapes. As we went northward I explained to Mistherd how he and his kind had been hoodwinked, used, made to live in a world that was never really there. I asked him if he wanted himself and whoever he cared about to go on till they died as domestic animals – yes, running in limited freedom on solid hills, but always called back to the dream-kennel.' His pipe fumed furiously. 'May I never see such bitterness again. He had been taught to believe he was free.'

Quiet returned, above the hectic traffic. Charlemagne drew nearer to setting; already the east darkened.

Finally Barbro asked, 'Do you know why?'

'Why children were taken and raised like that? Partly because it was in the pattern the Dwellers were creating; partly in order to study and experiment on members of our species – minds, that is, not bodies; partly because humans have special strengths which are helpful, like being able to endure full daylight.'

'But what was the final purpose of it all?'

Sherrinford paced the floor. 'Well,' he said, 'of course the ultimate motives of the aborigines are obscure. We can't do more than guess at how they think, let alone how they feel. But our ideas do seem to fit the data.

'Why did they hide from man? I suspect they, or rather their ancestors – for they aren't glittering elves, you know; they're mortal and fallible too – I suspect the natives were only being cautious at first, more cautious than human primitives, though certain of those on Earth were also slow to reveal themselves to strangers. Spying, mentally eavesdropping, Roland's Dwellers must have picked up enough language to get some idea of how different man was from them, and how powerful; and they gathered that more ships would be arriving, bringing settlers. It didn't occur to them that they might be conceded the right to keep their lands. Perhaps they're still more fiercely territorial than us. They determined to fight, in their own way. I daresay, once we begin to get insight into that mentality, our psychological science will go through its Copernican revolution.'

Enthusiasm kindled in him. 'That's not the sole thing we'll learn, either,' he went on. 'They must have science of their own, a nonhuman science born on a planet that isn't Earth. Because they did observe us as profoundly as we've ever observed ourselves; they did mount a plan against us, that would have taken another century or more to complete. Well, what else do they know? How do they support their civilization without visible agriculture or above-ground buildings or mines or anything? How can they breed whole new intelligent species to order? A million questions, ten million answers!'

'*Can* we learn from them?' Barbro asked softly. 'Or can we only overrun them as you say they fear?'

Sherrinford halted, leaned elbow on mantel, hugged his pipe and replied: 'I hope we'll show more charity than that to a defeated enemy. It's what they are. They tried to conquer us, and failed, and now in a sense we are bound to conquer them, since they'll have to make their peace with the civilization of the machine rather than see it rust away as they strove for. Still, they never did us any harm as atrocious as what we've inflicted on our fellow man in the past. And, I repeat, they could teach us marvelous things; and we could teach them, too, once they've learned to be less intolerant of a different way of life.'

'I suppose we can give them a reservation,' she said, and didn't know why he grimaced and answered so roughly:

'Let's leave them the honor they've earned! They fought to save the world they'd always known from that – ' he made a chopping gesture at the city – 'and just possibly we'd be better off ourselves with less of it.'

He sagged a trifle and sighed, 'However, I suppose if Elfland had won, man on Roland would at last – peacefully, even happily – have died away. We live with our archetypes, but can we live in them?'

Barbro shook her head. 'Sorry, I don't understand.'

'What?' He looked at her in a surprise that drove out melancholy. After a laugh: 'Stupid of me. I've explained this to so many politicians and scientists and commissioners and Lord knows what, these past days, I forgot I'd never explained to you. It was a rather vague idea of mine, most of the time we were traveling, and I don't like to discuss ideas prematurely. Now that we've met the Outlings and watched how they work, I do feel sure.'

He tamped down his tobacco. 'In limited measure,' he said, 'I've used an archetype throughout my own working life. The rational detective. It hasn't been a conscious pose – much – it's simply been an image which fitted my personality and professional style. But it draws an appropriate response from most people, whether or not they've ever heard of the original. The phenomenon is not uncommon. We meet persons who, in varying degrees, suggest Christ or Buddha or the Earth Mother or, say, on a less exalted plane, Hamlet or d'Artagnan. Historical, fictional, and mythical, such figures crystallize basic aspects of human psyche, and when we meet them in our real experience, our reaction goes deeper than consciousness.'

He grew grave again: 'Man also creates archetypes that are not individuals. The Anima, the Shadow – and, it seems, the Outworld. The world of magic, of glamour – which originally meant enchantment – of half-human beings, some like Ariel and some like Caliban, but each free of mortal frailties and sorrows – therefore, perhaps, a little carelessly cruel, more than a little tricksy; dwellers in dusk and moonlight, not truly gods but obedient to rulers who are enigmatic and powerful enough to be – Yes, our Queen of Air and Darkness knew well what sights to let lonely people see, what illusions to spin around them from time to time, what songs and legends to set going among them. I wonder how much she and her underlings gleaned from human fairy tales, how much they made up themselves, and how much men created all over again, all unwittingly, as the sense of living on the edge of the world entered them.'

Shadows stole across the room. It grew cooler and the traffic noises dwindled. Barbro asked mutedly: 'But what could this do?'

'In many ways,' Sherrinford answered, 'the outwayer *is* back in the dark ages. He has few neighbors, hears scanty news from beyond his horizon, toils to survive in a land he only partly understands, that may any night raise unforeseeable disasters against him and is bounded by enormous wildernesses. The machine civilization which brought his ancestors here is frail at best. He could lose it as the dark-age nations had lost Greece and Rome, as the whole of Earth seems to have lost it. Let him be worked on, long, strongly, cunningly, by the archetypical Outworld, until he has come to believe in his bones that the magic of the Queen of Air and Darkness is greater than the energy of engines: and first his faith, finally his deeds will follow her. Oh, it wouldn't happen fast. Ideally, it would happen too slowly to be noticed, especially by self-satisfied city people. But when in the end a hinterland gone back to the ancient way turned from them, how could they keep alive?'

Barbro breathed, 'She said to me, when their banners flew in the last of our cities, we would rejoice.'

'I think we would have, by then,' Sherrinford admitted. 'Nevertheless, I believe in choosing one's own destiny.'

He shook himself, as if casting off a burden. He knocked the dottle from his pipe and stretched, muscle by muscle. 'Well,' he said, 'it isn't going to happen.'

She looked straight at him. 'Thanks to you.'

A flush went up his thin cheeks. 'In time, I'm sure, somebody else would have – Anyhow, what matters is what we do next, and that's too big a decision for one individual or one generation to make.'

She rose. 'Unless the decision is personal, Eric,' she suggested, feeling heat in her own face.

It was curious to see him shy. 'I was hoping we might meet again.'

'We will.'


Ayoch sat on Wolund's Barrow. Aurora shuddered so brilliant, in such vast sheafs of light, as almost to hide the waning moons. Firethorn blooms had fallen; a few still glowed around the tree roots, amidst dry brok which crackled underfoot and smelled like woodsmoke. The air remained warm but no gleam was left on the sunset horizon.

'Farewell, fare lucky,' the pook called. Mistherd and Shadow-of-a-Dream never looked back. It was as if they didn't dare. They trudged on out of sight, toward the human camp whose lights made a harsh new star in the south.

Ayoch lingered. He felt he should also offer good-bye to her who had lately joined him that slept in the dolmen. Likely none would meet here again for loving or magic. But he could only think of one old verse that might do. He stood and trilled:

'Out of her breast
a blossom ascended.
The summer burned it.
The song is ended.'

Then he spread his wings for the long flight away.

# HOME

Like a bullet, but one that hunted its own target, the ferry left the mother ship and curved down from orbit. Stars crowded darkness, unwinking and wintry. Yakov Kahn's gaze went out the viewport over the pilot board, across thirty-three light-years to the spark which was Sol. Almost convulsively, he looked away again, sought the clotted silver of the Milky Way and the sprawl of Sagittarius. There, behind dust clouds where new suns were being born, lay the galaxy's heart.

Once he had dreamed of seeking thither himself. But he was a boy then, who stood on a rooftop and peered through city skyglow and city haze, wanting only to be yonder. Afterward the dream struck facts of distance, energy, and economics. The wreck had not gone under in an instant. His sons, his grandsons —

No. Probably no man ever would.

Beside him, Bill Redfeather's craggy features scowled at instruments. 'All systems check,' he reported.

Kahn's mouth twitched slightly upward. 'I should hope so.'

Redfeather looked irritated. It was the pilot's, not the co-pilot's, responsibility to be sure they wouldn't burn as a meteorite in the atmosphere of the planet.

Its night side swelled before them, a monstrous darkness when you remembered the lights of Earth, but rimmed to dayward with blue and rosy red. An ocean sheened, polished metal scutcheoned with a hurricane; and that was alien too, no pelagicultural cover, no floating towns or crisscrossing transport webs. As he watched how Kahn regarded the sight, Redfeather's mood turned gentle.

'You think too damn much, Jake,' he said.

'Well — ' Kahn shrugged. 'My last space trip.'

'Nonsense. They'll need men yet on the Lunar run.'

'A nice, safe shuttle.' Kahn's Israeli accent harshened his English. 'No, thank you. I will make a clean break and stay groundside. High time I began raising a family anyway.'

*If I can find a girl. Almost seventy years will have passed since we started out. And even then I was an anachronism, too many missions to too many stars . . . Cut that! No self-pity allowed.*

'I wonder what they've become like,' Redfeather said.

'Eh?' Kahn pulled himself out of his thoughts. 'Who?'

'The people, of course. A century here, cut off from the rest of the human race. That must have done things to them.'

Thus far the crew had talked little about what they would find. Too depressing. But evasion had to end. 'They will probably seem more familiar to you than to me,' Kahn said, 'being drawn from North America. Their radio reports haven't suggested any more social change than one would expect in a scientific base. A certain primitivism, I imagine; nothing else.'

'Even among nonhumans?'

'They don't appear to have been significantly influenced by their neighbors. Or vice versa, for that matter. Too large a difference. I should think the primary effect on them was due to Mithras itself.'

'How?'

'Room to move around. Wilderness. Horizons. But we will see.'

The ferry was coming into daylight now. Groombridge 1830 rose blindingly over the curve of its innermost planet. Clouds drifted gold across plains and great wrinkled mountains.

'Think we can get in some hunting and such?' Redfeather asked eagerly. 'I mean the real thing, not popping loose at a robot in an amusement park.'

'No doubt,' Kahn said. 'We will have time. They can't pack up and leave on no more notice than our call after we entered orbit.'

'Damned shame, to end the project,' Redfeather said. 'I hope they solved the rotation problem, anyhow.'

'Which?'

'You know. With the tidal action this sun must exert, why does Mithras have only a sixty-hour day?'

'Oh, that. That was answered in the first decade the base was here. I have read old reports. A smaller liquid core makes for less isostatic friction. Other factors enter in too, like the absence of a satellite. Trivial, compared to what they have been learning since. Imagine a biochemistry like Earth's, but with its own evolution, natives as intelligent as we are but not human, an entire *world*.'

Kahn's fist smote the arm of his chair. He bounced a little in his harness, under the low deceleration pressure. 'The Directorate is governed by idiots,' he said roughly. 'Terminating the whole interstellar program just because some cost accountant machine says population has grown so large and resources so low that we can't afford to keep on learning. My God, we can't afford not to! Without new knowledge, what hope have we for changing matters?'

'Could be the Directors had that in mind also,' Redfeather grunted.

Kahn gave the co-pilot a sharp glance. Sometimes Redfeather surprised him.


The houseboat came down the Benison River, past Riptide Straits, and there lay the Bay of Desire. The sun was westering, a huge red-gold ball that struck fire off the waters. Kilometers distant, on the opposite shore, the Princess reared her blue peak high over the clustered, climbing roofs of Withylet village; closer at hand, the sails of boats shone white as the wings of the sea whistlers cruising above them. The air was still warm, but through an open window David Thrailkill sensed a coolness in the breeze, and a smell of salt, off the Weatherwomb Ocean beyond the Door.

'Want to take the helm, dear?' he asked Leonie.

'Sure, if you'll mind Vivian,' said his wife.

Thrailkill went aft across the cabin to get a bottle of beer from the cooler. The engine throb was louder there, and didn't sound quite right. Well, an overhaul was overdue, after so long a time upriver. He walked forward again, with his seven-year-old daughter in tow. (That would have been three years on Earth, an enchanting age, though already he could see that she would have her mother's blond good looks and a touch of his own studiousness.) Leonie chuckled at them as they went by.

Strongtail was on the porch, to savor the view. They were following the eastern bayshore. It rose as steeply as the other side, in hills that were green from winter rains but had begun to show a tinge of summer's tawniness. Flameflowers shouted color among pseudograsses and scattered boskets. Thrailkill lowered his lanky form into a chair, cocked feet on rail, and tilted the bottle. Cold pungency gurgled past his lips, like water cloven by the twin bows. 'Ahhh!' he said. 'I'm almost sorry to come home.'

Vivien flitted in Strongtail's direction, several balls clutched to her chest. 'Juggle?' she begged.

'Indeed,' said the Mithran. The girl laughed for joy, and bounced around as much as the balls. Strongtail had uncommon skill in keeping things aloft and awhirl. His build helped, of course. The first expedition had compared the autochthones to kangaroos with bird heads and arms as long as a gibbon's. But a man who had spent his life among them needed no chimeras. To Thrailkill, his friend's nude, brown-furred small form was a unity, more graceful and in a way more beautiful than any human.

The slender beak remained open while Strongtail juggled, uttering those trills which men could not imitate without a vocalizer. 'Yes, a pleasant adventure,' he said. 'Fortune is that we have ample excuse to repeat it.'

'We sure do.' Thrailkill's gaunt face cracked in a grin. 'This is going to rock them back on their heels in Treequad. For nigh on two hundred and fifty years, we've been skiting across the world, and never dreamed about an altogether fantastic culture right up the Benison. *Won't* Painted Jaguar be surprised?'

He spoke English. After an Earth century of contact, the Mithrans around the Bay understood even if they were not able to voice the language. And naturally every human kid knew what the flutings of his playmates meant. You couldn't travel far, though, before you met strangeness: not surprising, on a planet whose most advanced civilization was pre-industrial and whose natives were nowhere given to exploration or empire building.

Sometimes Thrailkill got a bit exasperated with them. They were too damned gentle. Not that they weren't vigorous, merry, et cetera. You couldn't ask for a better companion than Strongtail. But he lacked ambition. He'd helped build this boat, and gone xenologizing on it, for fun and to oblige his buddy. When the mores of the riparian tribes became evident in all their dazzling complexities, he had not seen why the humans got so excited; to him, it was merely an occasion for amusement.

Thrailkill dismissed that recollection. *Mithras is their planet*, he reminded himself, not for the first time. *We're here simply because their ancestors were courteous enough to let our ancestors establish a base. If they seldom take any of the machines and ideas we offer, if they refuse chance after chance to really*

55

*accomplish something, that's their own affair. Maybe I just envy their attitude.*

'I do not grasp your last reference,' said Strongtail.

'Hm? Painted Jaguar? An old story among my people.' Thrailkill looked toward the sun, where it touched the haze around the Princess with amber. Earth's sun he had watched only on film, little and fierce and hasty in heaven. 'I'm not sure I understand it myself, quite.'

Point Desire hove in view, the closest thing to a city that the region possessed, several hundred houses with adobe walls and red tile roofs on a headland above the docks. A dozen or so boats were in, mainly trading ketches from the southern arm of the Bay.

'Anxious though I am to see my kindred,' the Mithran said, 'I think we would do wrong not to dine with Rich-in-Peace.'

Thrailkill laughed. 'Come off it, you hypocrite. You know damn well you want some of her cooking.' He rubbed his chin. 'As a matter of fact, so do I.'

The houseboat strode on. When it passed another craft, Strongtail exchanged cheerful whistles. That the blocky structure moved without sails or oars was no longer a cause of wonder, and never had been very much. The people took for granted that humans made curious things.

'Indeed this has been a delightful journey,' Strongtail mused. 'Morning mists rolling still and white, islands hidden among waterstalks, a fish line to trail aft, and at night our jesting in our own snug world . . . I would like a houseboat for myself.'

'Why, you can use this one any time,' Thrailkill said.

'I know. But so many kin and friends would wish to come with me, years must pass before they have each shared my pleasure. There should be at least one other houseboat.'

'So make one. I'll help whenever I get a chance, and you can have a motor built in Treequad.'

'For what fair value in exchange? I would have to work hard, to gather food or timber or whatever else the builder might wish.' Strongtail relaxed. 'No, too many other joys wait, ranging Hermit Woods, lazing on Broadstrands, making music under the stars. Or playing with your cub.' He sent the balls through a series of leaps that made Vivian squeal.

The boat eased into a berth. There followed the routine of making fast, getting shipshape, packing the stuff which must go ashore. That went quickly, because several Mithrans stopped their dockside fishing in order to help. They seemed agitated about something, but wouldn't say what. Presently everyone walked to the landward end of the dock. Planks boomed underfoot.

Rich-in-Peace's inn was not large, even by local standards, and few customers were present. Those sat on their tails at the counter, which had been split from a single scarletwood log, and talked with more excitement than usual. Leonie let the door screen fold behind her. 'Hello,' she called. 'We're back for some of your delicious chowder.'

'And beer,' Strongtail reminded. 'Never forget beer.'

Rich-in-Peace bustled around the counter. Her big amber eyes glistened. The house fell silent; this was her place, she was entitled to break the news.

'You have not heard?' she caroled.

'No, our radio went out on the way back.' Thrailkill replied. 'What's happened?'

She spread her hands. They had three fingers apiece, at right angles to each other. 'But so wonderful!' she exclaimed. 'A ship has come from your country. They say you can go home.' As if the implications had suddenly broken on her, she stopped. After a moment: 'I hope you will want to come back and visit us.'

*She doesn't realize,* flashed through the stupefaction in Thrailkill. He was only dimly aware of Leonie's tight grasp on his arm. *That's a one-way trip.*

Sunset smoldered away in bronze and gold. From the heights above Treequad, Kahn and Thrailkill could look past the now purple hills that flanked the Door, out to a glimpse of the Weatherwomb Ocean. The xenologist sighed. 'I always wanted to build a real seagoing schooner and take her there,' he said. 'Coasting down to Gate-of-the-South – what a trip!'

'I am surprised that the natives have not done so,' Kahn said. 'They appear to have the capability, and it would be better for trade than those toilsome overland routes you mentioned.'

'I suggested that, and my father before me,' Thrailkill answered. 'But none of them cared to make the initial effort. Once we thought about doing it ourselves, to set an example. But we had a lot of other work, and too few of us.'

'Well, if the natives are so shiftless, why do you care about improving their lot?'

Thrailkill bristled at the insult to his Mithrans, until he remembered that Kahn could not be expected to understand. ' "Shiftless" is the wrong word,' he said. 'They work as hard as

57

necessary. Their arts make everything of ours look sick. Let's just call them less adventurous than humans.' His smile was wry. 'Probably the real reason we've done so much here, and wanted to do so much more. Not for altruism, just for the hell of it.'

The mirth departed from him. He looked from the Door, past the twinkling lanterns of Goodwort and Withylet which guarded it, back across the mercury sheet of the Bay, to Treequad at his feet.

'So I'm not going to build that schooner,' he said. Roughly: 'Come on, we'd better return.'

They started downhill, over a trail which wound among groves of tall sweet-scented sheathbud trees. Leaves rustled in the twilight, a flock of marsh birds winged homeward with remote trumpetings, insects chirred from the pseudograsses. Below, Treequad was a darkness filling the flatlands between hills and Bay. Lights could be seen from windows, and the Center tower was etched slim against the waters; but the whole impression was of openness and peace, with some underlying mystery to which men could not quite put a name.

'Why did you establish yourselves here, rather than at the town farther north?' Kahn asked. His voice seemed flat and loud, and the way he jumped from subject to subject was also an offense to serenity. Thrailkill didn't mind, though. He had recognized his own sort of man in the dark, moody captain, which was why he had invited Kahn to stay with him and had taken his guest on this ramble.

*Good Lord, what can he do but grab blindly at whatever he notices? He left Earth a generation ago; and even if he read everything we sent up till then, why, we never could transmit more than a fraction of what we saw and heard and did. He's got two and a half – well, an Earth century's worth of questions to ask.*

Thrailkill glanced around. The eastern sky had turned plum color, where the first few stars trod forth. *We ourselves*, he thought, *have a thousand years' worth; ten thousand years'. But of course now those questions will never be asked.*

'Why Treequad?' he said slowly. 'Well, they already had a College of Poets and Ceremonialists here – call it the equivalent of an intellectual community, though in human terms it isn't very. They made useful go-betweens for us, in dealing with less well-educated natives. And then, uh, Point Desire is a trading center, therefore especially worth studying. We didn't want to disturb conditions by plumping our own breed down right there.'

'I see. That is also why you haven't expanded your numbers?'

'Partly. We'd like to. This continent, this whole planet, is so underpopulated that — But a scientific base can't afford to grow. How would everyone be brought home again when it's terminated?'

Fiercely: 'Damn you on Earth! You're terminating us too soon!'

'I agree,' Kahn said. 'If it makes any consolation, all the others are being ended too. They don't mind so greatly. This is the sole world we have found where men can live without carrying around an environmental shell.'

'What? There must be more.'

'Indeed. But how far have we ranged? Less than fifty light-years. And never visited half the stars in that radius. You don't know what a gigantic project it is, to push a ship close to the speed of light. Too gigantic. The whole effort is coming to an end, as Earth grows poor and weary. I doubt if it will ever be revived.'

Thrailkill felt a chill. The idea hadn't occurred to him before, in the excitement of meeting the ferriers, but — 'What can we do when we get there?' he demanded. 'We're not fitted for . . . for city life.'

'Have no fears,' Kahn said. 'Universities, foundations, vision programs, any number of institutions will be delighted to have you. At least, that was so when I left, and society appears to have gotten static. And you should have party conversation for the rest of your lives, about your adventures on Mithras.'

'M-m-m, I s'pose.' Thrailkill rehearsed some fragments of his personal years.

Adventure enough. When he and Tom Jackson and Gleam-of-Wings climbed the Snowtooths, white starkness overhead and the wind awhistle below them, the thunder and plumes of an avalanche across a valley, the huge furry beast that came from a cave and must be slain before it slew them. Or shooting the rapids on a river that tumbled down the Goldstream Hills, landing wet and cold at Volcano to boast over their liquor in the smoky-raftered tap-room of Monstersbane Inn. Prowling the alleys and passing the lean temples of the Fivedom; standing off a horde of the natives' half-intelligent, insensately ferocious cousins, in the stockade at Tearwort; following the caravans through the Desolations, down to Gate-of-the-South, while drums beat unseen from dry hills; or simply this last trip, along the Benison through fogs and waterstalks, to those lands where the dwellers gave their lives to nothing but rites that made no sense and one dared not laugh – Indeed Earth offered nothing like that, and the vision-screen people would pay well for a taste of it to spice their fantasies.

Though Thrailkill remembered quieter times more clearly, and did not see how they could be told. The Inn of the Poetess, small and snug beneath the stormcloud mass of Demon Mountain, firelight, songs, comradeship; shadows and sun-flecks and silence in Hermit Woods; sailing out to Fish Hound Island with Leonie on their wedding night, that the sunrise might find them alone on its crags (how very bright the stars had been – even little Sol was a beacon for them); afterward, building sand castles with Vivian on Broadstrands, while the surf rolled in from ten thousand kilometers of ocean. They used to end such a day by finding some odd eating place in Kings Point Station or Goodwort, and Vivian would fall asleep to the creak of the sweeps as their ferry trudged home across the water.

Well, those were private memories anyway.

He realized they had been walking for quite some time in silence. Only their footfalls on the cobbles, now that they were back in town, or an occasional trill from the houses that bulked on either side, could be heard. Courtesy insisted he should make conversation with the vaguely visible shape on his right. 'What will you do?' he asked. 'After we return, I mean.'

'I don't know,' Kahn said. 'Teach, perhaps.'

'Something technical, no doubt.'

'I could, if need be. Science and technology no longer change from generation to generation. But I would prefer history. I have had considerable time to read history, in space.'

'Really? I mean, the temporal contraction effect –'

'You forget that at one gravity acceleration, a ship needs a year to reach near-light speed, and another year to brake at the end. You passengers will be in suspended animation, but we of the crew must stand watch.'

Kahn lit a cigaret. Earlier, Thrailkill had experimented with one, but tobacco made him ill, he found. He wondered for a moment if Earth's food had the savor of Mithran. *Funny. I never appreciated kernelkraut or sour nuts or filet of crackler till now, when I'm about to lose them.*

The cigaret end brightened and faded, brightened and faded, like a tiny red watchlight in the gloaming. 'After all,' Kahn said, 'I have seen many human events. I was born before the Directorate came to power. My father was a radiation technician in the Solar War. And, too, mine are an old people, who spent most of their existence on the receiving end of history. It is natural that I should be interested. You have been more fortunate.'

'And the Mithrans are luckier yet, eh?'

'I don't know. Thus far, they are essentially a historyless race. Or are they? How can you tell? We look through our own eyes. To us, accomplishment equals exploitation of the world. Our purest science and art remain a sort of conquest. What might the Mithrans do yet, in Mithran terms?'

'Let us keep up the base,' Thrailkill said, 'and we'll keep on reporting what they do.'

'That would be splendid,' Kahn told him, 'except that there will be no ships to take your descendants home. You have maintained yourselves as an enclave of a few hundred people for a century. You cannot do so forever. If nothing else, genetic drift in that low a population would destroy you.'

They walked on unspeaking, till they reached the Center. It was a village within the village, clustered around the tower. Thence had sprung the maser beams, up through the sky to the relay satellite, and so to those on Earth who wondered what the universe was like. *No more,* Thrailkill thought. *Dust will gather, nightcats will nest in corroding instruments, legends will be muttered about the tall strangers who built and departed, and one century an earthquake will bring down this tower which talked across space, and the very myths will die.*

On the far side of the Mall, close to the clear plash of Louis' Fountain, they stopped. There lay Thrailkill's house, long and solid, made to endure. His grandfather had begun it, his father had completed it, he himself had wanted to add rooms but had no reason to when he would only be allowed two children. The windows were aglow, and he heard a symphony of Mithran voices.

'What the devil!' he said. 'We've got company.' He opened the door.

The fireplace danced with flames, against the evening cold. Their light shimmered off the beautiful grain of wainscots, glowed on patterned rugs and the copper statue which owned one corner, and sheened along the fur of his friends. The room was full of them: Strongtail, Gleam-of-Wings, Nightstar, Gift-of-God. Dreamer, Elf-in-the-Forest, and more and more, all he

61

had loved who could get here quickly enough. They sat grave on their tails, balancing cups of herb tea in their hands, while Leonie attended to the duties of a hostess.

She stopped when Thrailkill and Kahn entered. 'How late you are!' she said. 'I was growing worried.'

'No need,' Thrailkill replied, largely for Kahn's benefit. 'The last prowltiger hereabouts was shot five years ago.' *I did that. Another adventure — hai, what a stalk through the folded hills! (The Mithrans didn't like it. They attached some kind of significance to the ugly brutes. But prowltigers never took a Mithran. When the Harris boy was killed, we stopped listening to objections. Our friends forgave us eventually.)* He looked around. 'You honor this roof,' he said with due formalism. 'Be welcome in good cheer.'

Strongtail's music was a dirge. 'Is the story true that you can never return?'

'Yes, I'm afraid so,' Thrailkill said. Aside to Kahn: 'They want us to stay. I'm not sure why. We haven't done anything in particular for them.'

'But you tried,' said Nightstar. 'That was a large plenty, that you should care.'

'And you were something to wonder at,' Elf-in-the-Forest added.

'We have enjoyed you,' Strongtail said. 'Why must you go?'

'We took council,' sang Gift-of-God, 'and came hither to ask from house to house that you remain.'

'But we can't!' Leonie's words cracked over.

'Why can you not?' responded Dreamer.

It burst upon Thrailkill. He stood in the home of his fathers and shouted: 'Why not? We can!'


The long night drew toward a close. Having slept, Kahn borrowed one of the flitters that had been manufactured here and went after Bill Redfeather, who'd gone on a jaunt with one of the autochthons.

He hummed across the Bay under constellations not so different from those of Earth. Thirty-three light-years were hardly significant in the galaxy. But the humans no longer used human names; those were the Boat, the Garden of Healing, the Fourfold, that wheeled and glittered around another pole star. *I suppose there are more native influences,* he thought. *Not too many, but some. I wonder what kind of civilization they would build. They could hardly help but do better than Earth, on a rich and uncrowded planet. In time they would be able to launch starships of their own.*

The unrolling map guided him toward Starkbeam, and when the hamlet came into sight he detected the emissions from Redfeather's portable transceiver and homed on them. They led him to a peak that loomed over the peninsular hills and the soaring scarletwood forest. He must come down vertically on a meadow.

Dew soaked his breeches as he stepped out. The eastern sky had paled, but most light still came from the stars, and from the campfire that fluttered before a tent. Redfeather and Strongtail squatted there, half seen in shadows. A pot on a framework of sticks bubbled above, merrily competing with the first sleepy bird-chirps. The air was raw, and Kahn shivered and felt glad to settle down with hands held near the coals.

Strongtail murmured some notes. 'I think that means "welcome",' Redfeather said. Strongtail nodded. 'Breakfast will be ready soon. Or lunch or something. Hard to get used to this diurnal period. What do the base people do?'

'About twenty hours awake, ten asleep, around the clock,' Kahn said. 'Have you had a good outing?'

'Lord, yes! Strongtail's a mighty fine guide, even if he can't talk to me. Very kind of you to take me.' Strongtail trilled in pleasure. 'I do wish I could hunt, but my pal here doesn't quite approve. Oh, well, I'm glad to get out in the woods anyway.' Redfeather stirred the pot. 'I suppose you're joining us?'

'No, that wasn't why I called.' Kahn lit a cigaret and smoked in short, hard puffs. 'Business. Regrets, but you will have to come directly back with me.'

'Huh? What's the rush? I mean, unless the people changed their minds about staying.'

'No, they haven't. They have been threshing the matter this whole night. Hardly any of them wish to leave with us. I argued, but I might as well have talked to those trees.'

'Why bother, Jake? We don't have positive orders to bring them back.' Redfeather smiled. 'Give me a few days here, and I could well decide to stay myself.'

'What?' Kahn stared at the firelit face. 'Yes, I see. I am not personally one for the bucolic life – '

'No need to be. Having made the final decision, we . . . they'll want mines, factories, sawmills, everything you can name.'

Kahn glanced at Strongtail. 'What do you say to that?' he asked. 'Do you wish these things done?'

The Mithran nodded slowly. A qualified 'Yes', Khan assumed; he didn't like the idea, but various regions could be given the humans and there was plenty of room elsewhere. If, indeed, anything that formal was contemplated. Thrailkill had remarked that the autochthons had no concept of real estate as property.

Kahn finished his cigaret, ground out the stub with a vicious gesture, and rose. 'Excuse me, Strongtail,' he said. 'We have private affairs to discuss. Come into the flitter, Bill.'

Privacy was another notion, incomprehensible, with which Strongtail cooperated to oblige. He tended the pot, drank in its odors and the green scent of the awakening forest, was briefly saddened by the trouble he had sensed, and then turned his mind to more easy and pleasurable thoughts. Once he started. Kahn's yell pierced the flitter canopy. 'God damn you, I am the captain and you will obey orders!' He knew that humans often submitted themselves, however reluctantly, to the will of someone else. The fact that Mithrans left a job whenever they got bored had occasioned friction in the early days. Later generations solved the problem by rarely employing Mithrans.

Well-a-day, they made up for their peculiarities by such things as houseboats. It would be amusing, no, wonderful to see what they did when they really felt themselves part of the land.

Unless – No, while the prowltiger episode, and certain others, had been unfortunate, limits were not exceeded. Should that ever happen, Strongtail would be forced to kill. But he would continue to love as he did.

The canopy slid back and the Earthmen returned. Kahn looked grim, Redfeather was quiet and shaken. Sweat filled his brows. 'I'm sorry,' he told the Mithran, 'I must go to the spaceship.'


The meeting hall in Treequad was so big that the entire human population could gather within. Mounting the stage, Kahn looked beyond gaily muraled walls to the faces. The very graybeards, he thought, had an air of youth which did not exist for any age on Earth. Sun and wind had embraced them throughout their lives. They had had a planet to wander in, as men had not owned since Columbus.

He turned to Thrailkill, who had accompanied him. Normally an elected speaker presided over these sessions, but today they listened to him and naturally his host went along. 'Is everybody here?' he asked.

Thrailkill's gaze swept the room. Sunlight streamed in the windows, to touch women's hair and men's eyes with ruddiness. A quiet had fallen, underscored by rustlings and shufflings. Somewhere a baby cried, but was quickly soothed.

'Yes,' he said. 'The last field expedition came in two hours ago, from the Icefloe Dwellers.' He scowled at Kahn. 'I don't know why you want this assembly. Our minds are made up.'

The spaceman consulted his watch. He had to stall for a bit. His men wouldn't get down from orbit for some minutes yet, and then they must walk here. 'I told you,' he said. 'I want to make a final appeal.'

'We've heard your arguments,' Thrailkill said.

'Not formally.'

'Oh all right,' Thrailkill advanced to the lectern. The PA boomed his words forth under the rafters.

'The meeting will please come to order,' he said. 'As you know, we're met for the purpose of officially ratifying the decision that we have reached. I daresay Captain Kahn will need such a recorded vote. First he'd like to address you.' He bowed slightly to his guest and took a chair. Leonie was in the front row with Vivian; he winked at them.

Kahn leaned on the stand. His body felt heavy and tired. 'Ladies and gentlemen,' he said, 'you have spent many hours this past night talking things over in private groups. Quite an exciting night, no? I have asked you to come here after sleeping on the question, because your choice should be made in a calmer mood, it being irrevocable.

'Hardly any of you have agreed to leave with us. I wonder if the majority have considered what their own desires mean. As was said long ago, "Il faut vouloir les consequences de ce que l'on veut." ' Blankness met him, driving home how far these people had drifted from Earth. 'I mean you must want the results of what you want. You are too few to maintain a culture at the modern level. True, your ancestors brought along the means to produce certain amenities, and you have a lot of information on microtape. But there are only so many heads among you, and each head can hold only so much. You are simply not going to have enough engineers, medical specialists, psychopediatricians, geneticists . . . every trained type necessary to operate a civilization, as opposed to a mere scientific base. Some of your children will die from causes that could have been prevented. Those who survive will mature ignorant of Earth's high heritage.

'A similar thing happened before, on the American frontier. But America was close to Europe. The new barbarism ended in a few generations, as contact strengthened. You will be alone, with no more than one thin thread of radio, a lifetime passing between message and answer. Do you want to sink back into a dark age?'

Someone called, 'We've done okay so far.' Others added remarks. Kahn was content to let them wrangle; thus he gained time, without drawing on his own exhausted resources. But Thrailkill shushed them and said:

'I believe we're aware of that problem, Captain. In fact, we've lived with it during the whole existence of this . . . Colony.' *There,* Kahn thought. *He spoke the word.* 'We haven't really been bothered. From what we hear about Earth, we've gained more than we've lost.' Applause. 'And now that you've made us realize this is our home, this is where we belong, why, we won't stay small. For purely genetic reasons we'll have to expand our population as fast as possible. My wife and I always did want a houseful of kids. Now we can have them.' Cheering began. His reserve broke apart. 'We'll build our own civilization! And someday we'll come back to you, as visitors. You're giving up the stars. We're not!'

They rose from their chairs and shouted.

Kahn let the noise surf around him, while he stood slumped. *Soon,* he begged. *Let it be soon.* Seeing that he remained where he was, the crowd grew gradually still. He waited till the last one had finished talking to his neighbor. Then the silence was so deep that he could hear the songbirds outside.

'Very well,' he said in a dull tone. 'But what is to become of the Mithrans?'

Thrailkill, who had also stayed on his feet, said rapidly, 'You mentioned that to me before, Captain. I told you then and I tell you now, the planet has room for both races. We aren't going to turn on our friends.'

'My mate Bill Redfeather is an Amerind,' Kahn said. 'Quite a few of his ancestors were friends to the white man. It didn't help them in the long run. I am a Jew myself, if you know what that means. My people spent the better part of two thousand years being alien. We remember in our bones how that was. Finally some started a country of their own. The Arabs who were there objected, and lived out the rest of their lives in

66

refugee camps. Ask Muthaswamy, my chief engineer, to explain the history of Moslem and Hindu in India. Ask his assistant Ngola to tell you what happened when Europe entered Africa. And, as far as that goes, what happened when Europe left again. You cannot intermingle two cultures. One of them will devour the other. And already, this minute, yours is the more powerful.'

They mumbled, down in the hall, and stared at him and did not understand. He sucked air into his lungs and tried anew:

'Yes, you don't intend to harm the Mithrans. Thus far there has been little conflict. But when your numbers grow, when you begin to rape the land for all the resources this hungry civilization needs, when mutual exasperation escalates into battle — can you speak for your children? Your grandchildren? Their grandchildren, to the end of time? The people of Bach and Goethe brought forth Hitler. No, you don't know what I am talking about, do you?

'Well, let us suppose that man on this planet reverses his entire previous record and gives the natives some fairly decent reservations and does not take them away again. Still, how much hope have they of becoming anything but parasites? They cannot become one with you. The surviving Amerinds could be assimilated, but they were human. Mithrans are not. They do not and cannot think like humans. But don't they have the right to live in their world as they wish, make their own works, hope their own hopes?

'You call this planet underpopulated. By your standards, that is correct. But not by the natives'. How many individuals per hectare do you expect an economy like theirs to support? Take away part of a continent, and you murder that many unborn sentient beings. But you won't stop there. You will take the world, and so murder an entire way of existence. How do you know that way isn't better than ours? Certainly you have no right to deny the universe the chance that it is better.'

They seethed and buzzed at his feet. Thrailkill advanced, fists clenched, and said flatly, 'Have you so little pride in being a man?'

'On the contrary,' Kahn answered, 'I have so much pride that I will not see my race guilty of the ultimate crime. We are not going to make anyone else pay for our mistakes. We are going home and see if we cannot amend them ourselves.'

'So you say!' Thrailkill spat.

*O God of mercy, send my men.* Kahn looked into the eyes

of the one whose salt he had eaten, and knew they would watch him for what remained of his life. And behind would gleam the Bay of Desire, and the Princess' peak holy against a smokeless heaven, and the Weather-womb waiting for ships to sail west. 'You will be heroes on Earth,' he said. 'And you will at least have memories. I – '

The communicator in his pocket buzzed 'Ready.' He slapped it once: 'Go ahead.'

Thunder crashed on the roof, shaking walls. A deep-toned whistle followed. Kahn sagged back against the lectern. That would be the warboat, with guns and nuclear bombs.

The door flew open. Redfeather entered, and a squad of armed men. The rest had surrounded the hall.

Kahn straightened. His voice was a stranger's, lost in the yells and cries: 'You are still citizens of the Directorate. As master of an official ship, I have discretionary police authority. Will or no, you shall come back with me.'

He saw Leonie clutch her child to her. He ducked Thrailkill's roundhouse swing and stumbled off the stage, along the aisle toward his men. Hands grabbed at him. Redfeather fired a warning burst, and thereafter he walked alone. He breathed hard, but kept his face motionless. It wouldn't do for him to weep. Not yet.

# THE ALIEN ENEMY

Winter darkness falls early on Rotterdam. When my flitter had parked, I walked to a parapet and saw light in star clusters, nebulae, comet tails, filling the spaces of the city. Windows were blinking out in the offices, where towers lifted row on row from the waterfront. But vehicles swarmed, signs danced, shops beckoned, the pavements made a luminous web as far inland as I could see – it appeared to flicker with the ground traffic that counted endless rosaries along it – and the harbor and canals interwove a softer sheen. I was too high to make out people through all that gloom and glow. They were melted into a mere humanity, and their voices came to me as the distant surf of machines.

Up here was less illumination, just some tubes around the lanes and walkways, a fluorescent door to the elevator head, and whatever spilled down from the beacon. So although the air was raw and damp in my nostrils, forcing my hands into tunic pockets, I could look past the electric star which marks this building, out to a few of the real stars. Orion was aloft and the Charles Wain stood on its head over the Pole. I shivered and wished the Ministry of Extraterrestrial Affairs had picked some other place for a centrum, an island farther south where the constellations bloom after dark like flowers.

But even the Directorate has to make compromises. The desirable places on Earth filled up long ago, and then the less desirable, and then the undesirable, until the only clear horizons left are on the mountain roofs, the icecaps, the stone-and-sand deserts, whatever is still worse to make a living from than the bottom of a megalopolis. The bureaucrats I work for did not do so badly; the Low Countries complex has much to recommend it. They control a lot of wealth and are correspondingly influential.

Anyway, I don't have to live in Rotterdam, except a few days at a time, reporting in or getting briefed. Otherwise I mostly spend my furloughs at one or another resort, as expensive and exclusive as possible. Thus I needn't observe what man has inflicted on this planet his mother while I was gone. Spaceman's pay accumulates wonderfully on the long hauls, years or decades in a stretch. I can afford whatever I want on Earth: even clean air, trees, a brook to drink from, a deer to glimpse, unlighted nights when I take a girl out and show her the stars I have visited.

Let me see, I thought, once this is over with here, where should I go? Hitherto I've avoided places where Cumae is visible. But why, really? Hm . . . catalogued HR 6806, 33.25 light years distant, K2 dwarf of luminosity 0.62 Sol . . . yes, I'll want a small telescope as well as some large brags for the girl . . .

One star detached itself and whirred toward me. Startled, I realized that this must be Tom Brenner coming. Suddenly I was in no more mood to brag about what I had done at Cumae than I was on first returning. I didn't want to confront him, especially alone. If I hurried, I could be inside before he set down. I could await him together with d'Indre, impregnable in the apparatus of government.

But no. I had seen too much – we had both seen too much, he and I, and all those men and women and children for whom he must speak tonight – on the high plains of his planet. In our very separate ways, we had both known the terror of the alien enemy. I could never be totally an official to him. So I stayed by the parapet, waiting. The breath came out of me like smoke and the cold crept inside.

On Sibylla it was always hot. Cumae glowers half again as great in the sky of that world as Sol does on Earth, and pours down nearly twice the energy. Those wavelengths are poor in ultra-violet but rich in infrared. The sunlight is orange-tinted, not actually furnace color though it feels that way.

I asked Brenner why the colonists didn't move upward. Peaks shouldered above the horizon. Their snows were doubly bright against the purplish heaven, doubly beautiful against the gray-green bushland that stretched around us, murmurous and resinous under a dry wind. I saw that timberline, or whatever passed for it, reached almost to the tops. The dark, slightly iridescent hues suggested denser growth than here. Yonder must be a well-watered country, fertile in soil, and cool, cool.

'Not enough air,' he said. He spoke English, with a faint American twang remaining after generations. They were chiefly

Americans who went to Sibylla. 'We're about as high on this massif as we can go.'

'But . . . oh, yes,' I recalled. 'The pressure gradient's steeper than on Earth. Your planet's got fifty percent more diameter, a third more surface gravity.'

'And less air to start with.' Brenner cleared his throat. I recognized the preliminary to a speech.

'We leave the lowlands be because they're too hot, not because of too thick an atmosphere,' he said. 'Remember, this is a metal-poor globe, lowish density in spite of its mass. So it didn't out-gas as much as it might have, in the beginning. Also, on account of the slow rotation, it don't have any magnetic field worth mentioning. Cumae may not be the liveliest star in the universe, but it does spit plenty protons and photons and stuff to thin out an atmosphere that hasn't got a magnetic field to hide behind. We get a pretty strong radiation background too, for the same reason; gives medical problems, and it'd be worse higher up. Furthermore, when you got an extra ought-point-three gee on you, and manual labor to do, you need lots of oxygen. So the long and the short of it is, we can't colonize the real heights.' He cocked his head at me. 'Didn't they brief you ay-tall, son?'

I looked back at him hard, feeling I rated more respect as the first officer of an exploratory ship. His leathery features crinkled in a slow grin. The President of Sibylla was no more formal than the rest of his ten thousand people.

He wore the usual archaic kilts, blouse, boots, sun helmet set rakishly on his grizzled head, machete at hip. But my uniform was less neat than his garb, ten minutes after we had left the buggy by the roadside and started climbing. The gravity didn't bother me; we use rougher accelerations on a craft like the *Bering*. I was aware of my flesh and bones dragging downward, nothing worse. The heat, though, the booming and thrusting wind, the scanted lungfuls I breathed, dryness afire in nose and throat, malignant grab of branches and slither of sandy soil, something faintly intoxicant about the plant odors, had entered me. I was sweat-drenched, dusty, a-gasp and a-tremble, and gladder than I should be of a chance to rest.

I decided not to stand on the dignity I didn't have. Besides, I thought, we were men together in the face of the not human. It had killed, it could kill again, it could smite Earth herself. I felt lonelier in that wide grim landscape than ever between the stars.

'They gave us what information was available,' I said. 'But it

71

was simultaneously too ample – for one head to contain – and too little – for the totality of a world. Hard for us to guess what's significant and what's incidental. And you've been isolated from us for nearly two centuries. Nothing but a thread of laser contact, with a third of each century needed to cross the distance between. Our fleet took longer still, of course; the big ships aren't meant to go above one gee, so they need a year to approach light speed and another year to decelerate. Inboard time at minimum tau factor isn't negligible either. We experienced several months in covering those parsecs. And we were wondering the whole way if we'd arrive to find the aliens had returned – arrive to find you dead here and a trap set for us. Under the circumstances, sir, we were bound to forget some of what we'd learned.'

'Well, yes, I reckon you would at that,' Brenner said. 'Getting back to why we've settled this Devil's Meadows district, I can tell you we haven't got any better place, and most are not as good. Sibylla is not Earth and never will be.'

'But you have colonized the polar regions, haven't you? The original expedition team suggested it, and my briefing said – '

'We abandoned them a spell back. They do have higher air pressure and lower background count, at a reasonable average temperature. But that's only an average. Don't you forget, the rotation period is locked to two-thirds of the year, we being so close to the sun. Sixty-five Earthdays of light are tolerable, though it gets too hot toward evening for us to work. We can grow crops, sort of, with lamps to help through the sixty-five-day night. But at the poles, a thirty-seven-degree axial tilt, the seasons are too flinkin' extreme. What with everything else they had going against them, our poor little terrestrial plants kept dying off there. We haven't the industry or the resources to practice greenhouse agriculture on the needful scale.' Brenner shrugged. 'Finally we gave up and everybody moved equatorward.'

I glanced down the crater slope. The road from Jimstown was dirt, a track nearly lost to sight, rutted, overgrown in places, little used since the destruction of New Washington. But traffic had never been heavy along it; no community on Sibylla was ever more than an overgrown village, and most were less. Tiny at this remove stood Brenner's buggy. The lank horse sniffed discouragedly at the brush it could not eat.

We might have taken a flitter from one of the relief ships. But that would have meant waiting until it could be unloaded and fetched down from orbit. Besides, I had wanted some feel of

72

what Sybilla and its people were really like.

I was getting it.

High hopes, two hundred years ago. People who were going to an uncrowded unplundered world, a whole new world, and this time build things right. They understood there would be hardship, danger, strangeness, on a planet for which our kind of life is not really fitted. But there would be nothing that men had not encountered and overcome elsewhere. The explorers had made certain of that beforehand.

Economics was a stronger motive than decency for being sure. The Directorate takes a bit of political pressure off itself with each colony it establishes, but does not really solve any physical problems at home; and the cost of sending the big ships is fantastic. The aim is to make Earth's people look up through the dust and smoke and say, 'Well, at least somebody's doing all right out there, and maybe we'll be picked to go in the next emigration, if we stay in favor with the authorities meanwhile.' Failures would be very, very upsetting. Only the news of outright attack had justified organizing the Colonial Fleet to evacuate the Sibyllans.

The investment in them was so huge. Their ancestors came with tools, machinery, chemicals, seeds, suspense-frozen animal embryos, scientific gear . . . the basics. Of course, they brought a full stock of technical references too. As population expanded, they would build fusion power stations, they would replace the native life forms in ever larger areas with terrene species, they would at last create Paradise. To judge from their laser reports, they had been following out the plan. It was going slowly, because Sibylla was uncommonly hostile, but it was going.

Now – the reasons why they had not rebuilt were plain to see. The lean ships that appeared in the sky, sixty-eight years ago, bombing and flaming, had knocked the foundations out from under the colony. Too much plant was wrecked, too many lives were lost, too few resources were left. For a lifetime, the people could merely hang on, keep their economy stumbling along at a seventeenth- or eighteenth-century level, cling to the hope that we would answer their appeal. And all the while they knew fear.

I looked again at Tom Brenner. Before he was born, the enemy aliens had destroyed from pole to pole. In days – Earth-days – their fleet had departed back into unknownness. At any instant they might return, and not be content with blowing his toy towns off the map. I wondered how deep the weariness went that I read upon him. Yet he stood straight, and he had a squinty-eyed grin, and two of his children had survived to adulthood and one grandchild was alive and healthy.

'Come on,' I said in a harshened voice. 'Let's get this finished.'

We didn't stop till we mounted the rim and looked down into the fused black bowl where New Washington had been. A few skeletons of buildings jutted from the edges, but only a few, their frameworks grotesquely twisted. I estimated that the blast had released fifty megatons.

The star became a taxi. It glided to a halt across the deck from me and balanced while the stocky figure climbed out. I wondered how he paid it. They had told me the Sibyllans were interned on a military reservation while the Director and his cabinet decided what to do about them. Well, when d'Indre demanded a live conference with the old man, perhaps the colonel had taken pity and slipped him some munits so he could arrive like a citizen, not a consignment.

The taxi took off. Brenner started toward the door. At home he had walked with a rolling, ursine gait. Here he flowstepped, light and easy as an Earthdweller on Mars. His cloak flapped loose, his singlet was open on the broad hairy chest. The unaccustomed cold didn't seem to bother him, rather he savored it.

I moved to intercept him. 'Good evening,' I said.

Shadows barred our faces. He leaned forward to peer at me. The cigar dropped from his jaws. 'Holy hopping Judas – Nick Simić!' He shook his head in bewilderment. 'But you, your ship, you stayed behind.'

'Your settlement was out of touch with astronautics,' I said. My tone was sharper than intended; I really wanted to gentle the shock for him. 'The Colonial Fleet accelerates at one gee. But in an exploratory vessel like the *Bering*, we're selected professionals; and the motors have a lot less mass to act on. We load ourselves with gravanol and crank her up as high as ten gees. In five or six weeks we're close to light speed and can ease off. I've been home for a year.'

'You, uh, didn't stay long on Sibylla, then.'

'Long enough.'

'Well.' He straightened. The remembered chuckle sounded in his throat. 'Quite a surprise, son, quite a surprise. But pleasant.' He thrust out his hand. I took it. His clasp was firm. 'And how are your shipmates?'

'Very well, thank you, the last I saw. The *Bering* has left again. Further study of the Delta Eridani System. The third planet looks promising, but its ecology is peculiar and – ' I realized I was chattering to avoid speaking truth. 'I stayed,' I said, 'since I was in charge of our investigation on the ground and drafted our report. Citizen d'Indre wanted me for a consultant when you arrived.'

'I'm sorry if you missed going on account of us.'

'No matter. I'm in line for a command of my own.' That was true, but I said it merely to cheer him a little. 'How are your people doing?'

'Okay to date.' Brenner didn't seem in need of consolation, now that he had gotten over his surprise. I don't suppose anyone grew old on Sibylla who couldn't land on his feet when the floor caved in. He drew a breath and gave that straight-in-the-eye look which he had once described as Horsetrader's Honest Expression Number Three. ' 'Course,' he said, 'we wonder a wee bit why we're held incommunicado and till when.'

'That has to be decided,' I said. 'What happens tonight could be pivotal.'

'Don't the proles know we're here?'

'Nothing except rumors. Your story has to be handled like fulminate. You can't imagine how restless those billions there are.' My hand swept an arc around the city. It growled and grumbled. 'The original news, nonhuman vessels attacking Sibylla, was let out with infinite care, and only because it couldn't be suppressed. Considering that they seemed to have faster-than-light travel, and something like gravity control, the way you told it, the photographs you transmitted – Panic can bring riot, insurrection.' I paused. 'So can rage.'

'Um. Yeh.' The lines deepened around Brenner's mouth, but somehow he kept his tone easy. 'Well, what say we get on with it? . . . Oh, almost forgot.' He stooped to pick up the cigar. 'Soldier gave me some o' these. Friendly taste. No tobacco on our planet, you recall. We'd everything we could do to raise enough food to keep alive.'

My gullet tightened. 'Put that thing away!' I exclaimed. 'Over the side with it! Don't you understand who we're about to see? Jules d'Indre, Minister of Extraterrestrial Affairs. What he recommends be done about you, the Director is almost sure to decree. I warn you, Brenner, be careful!'

He regarded me a while before he obeyed. His next words were astonishing. 'Did that girl who traveled with you, Laurie MacIver, did she ship out in the *Bering*?'

'Why, yes.'

'Too bad.' He spoke softly, and for a moment laid his hand on my shoulder. 'I think you want to help us, son, according to your lights. But she had something extra. You know the word *simpático*?'

I nodded. 'She is that,' I agreed.

We went ranging about, she and I, after a ground-effect car had been brought down and assembled. My thought was to interview as many Sibyllans as possible before they left. None were alive who had experienced the attack, but older ones might recollect what the generation before them had said, and might have noticed significant things in the bombed-out towns. before salvage and erosion blurred the clues. Laurie accompanied me for several reasons. We didn't need a computer officer here, and you don't travel alone on another planet. But primarily, she understood people, she listened, and they talked freely because they sensed that she cared.

It is not true what the alleydwellers snigger, that spacewomen are nothing but a convenience for spacemen. They hold down responsible posts. And in the black ocean between stars, among the deaths that lair on every new world, on return to an Earth grown strange, you need someone very special.

Just the same, we had thin luck. Sunset handicapped us. Cumae hung low and went lower, casting an inflamed light that was hard to see by across the plateaus. But the air had cooled sufficiently for outdoor work, and everyone on those pitiful farms toiled till he dropped in his tracks. They must complete their daylight jobs – discing and sowing at the present season, plus hay harvest, livestock roundup, and I don't know what else – largely with muscle power. They could only illuminate a limited part of their holdings after the moonless dark came upon them, truck gardens and such that would fail otherwise. Metal and manpower were too scarce to produce the factories which could have produced the machines and energy sources they lacked.

To be sure, this was the last round for them. They were going to Earth. But you can't spaceload ten thousand human beings overnight. The Fleet was barely able to carry the rations they would need on their journey. They must feed themselves meanwhile, and they had no reserves. I was appalled at the wretched yields, the scrawny animals, the stunted timber. And, while most of the individuals I saw were whipcord tough, they were undersized, they had few living children, the graveyards were broad and filled.

'Terrene life is so marginal here,' Laurie said as we drove. Her voice was muted with compassion. We had no logical need for a recital of the facts. We had known them since before we left Earth, when we studied the reports of communications from Sibylla. But those were words. Here she met the reality. She needed to put it back into words for herself, before she could reach beyond the anguish and think about practical ways to help.

'Not simply that the native species are poisonous to us,' she said. 'They poison the soil for our crops. You have to keep weeds, bacteria, everything out of a field for years before the rain's leached it to the point where you can begin building a useful ecology. And then it's apt to be attacked by something – new poisons seeping in, diseases, stormwinds – and at best, it never gets strongly established.'

I nodded and listed the causes, to hold off the idea of a personally evil cosmos. 'Long nights, weird seasons, shortage of several trace elements, ultraviolet poverty coupled with X-ray and particle irradiation, gravity tending to throw terrene fluid balances out of kilter, even the geological instability. Some of their best mines collapsed in earthquakes in the early days, did you know? – and never could be reopened. Oh, yes, it's a hard world for humans.'

My fist struck the control panel and I said with a barren anger: 'But so are the others. There's nothing wrong here that men haven't found, and beaten. The wildlife is worse on Zion, the weight is heavier on Atlas, a full-fledged ice age is under way on Asgard, Lucifer is hotter and has a higher particle count – '

She turned in her seat to face me. Sundown light, streaming through the turret, changed her gold hair to copper against purple shadows. 'But none of those were attacked,' she said.

'Not yet,' I said. 'At least, as far as we know.'

We should not have mentioned it. The thought had haunted us since we returned from our last voyage and got the news. It dwelt in the back of every mind on Earth. Perhaps it had done so since man first ventured beyond the Solar System. Our few score parsecs of exploring are no trail whatsoever into that wilderness which is the galaxy. Who can doubt that others prowl it, with longer legs and sharper fangs? Who's next?

Why had they struck? How? Where else? *Who's next?*

The Sibyllans did their best to answer Laurie's questions and mine. But not only were they hard-pressed for time and dull-witted with exhaustion, their information was scant. I had now inspected the ruins, some photographs of ships in flight, eye-witness accounts, compiled histories. The basic narrative was in my brain.

The raiders could not hit everywhere at once. Josiah Brenner, Tom's father, President in his day, got most population centers evacuated before they went up in fireballs. A majority already lived on isolated farms, it took so many hectares to support one person. For the same reason, the former townsfolk scattered across the whole habitable planet afterward.

The result was that hardly anyone today knew anything that I did not. In fact, my picture of the catastrophe was clearer than most. The ordinary Sibyllan had neither time nor energy for studying the past. The educational level had plummeted; children generally left school to work before they were twelve Earth-years old. Folklore took the place of books.

The books themselves were vague. No real census or scholarship was possible. 'Casualties were heavy,' said the chroniclers, and told many tales of suffering and heroism. But the figures they gave were obvious guesswork, often contradicting someone else's. I believed I could make a better estimate myself on the basis of one fact. The Sibyllan population which the original colonizing scheme had projected for this decade was some two hundred thousand. The actual population was a twentieth of that.

After a while, Laurie and I quit. We could do more good back in Jimstown, helping prepare for the exodus. With facilities as primitive as they were here, that was going to be a harrowing job. Our crew would stay after the Fleet left and search for further clues. Besides, I didn't fancy traveling after dark.

We had to, though. Passing near a scarp, our car was struck by a boulder when the crust shivered and started a landslide. The damage took hours to fix – in that smoldering light and abominable wind. We could have called for a flitter, but that would have meant leaving the car till dawn. It might be totally wrecked, and it could ill be spared. We drove on.

Cumae went under the mountains. Night thickened as clouds lifted. Presently it was absolute, except where our headlights speared before us, picking out bushes that tossed in the wind and occasional three-eyed animals that slunk between them. The air grew louder, thrusting against the sides, making them quiver

78

and resonate, until the noise filled our skulls. Then the rain came, a cloudburst such as Earth has never seen, mixed with hail like knucklebones.

'We'd better take shelter!' I yelled. Laurie could barely hear me through the drumbeat and the howling. 'High ground – get away from flash floods – ' Lightning blinded me; the whole heaven was incandescent, again and again and again, and thunder picked me up and shook me. I strained over the charts, the intertial navigator, yes, this way, a farmstead . . .

We could not have made it on wheels. The ground effect held us above mudslides, water avalanches, flattened crops and splintered orchards. Barely, it held us, though the hurricane tried to fling us back into the rising river which had been a valley. I do not know how long it was before we found the cottage, save that it was long indeed.

The house stood. Like most dwellings on Sibylla, it was a fortress, rock walls, shuttered slit windows, ponderous doors, roof held down by cables. In thin air, driven by high temperature differentials and solar irradiations, you must expect murderous weather from time to time. The barns were smashed, there having been insufficient manpower and materials to build them as sturdily, and no doubt the cattle and crops were lost. But the house stood.

I reached its lee, threw out a couple of ground anchors, put the autopilot on standby, and opened the escape hatch. Laurie slipped, the wind caught her, she almost went downhill to her death. I grabbed her, though, got dragged into the mud but hung on somehow. Clinging together, we fought our way through a universe of storm to the house. The door was bolted from within. Our pounding was lost in the racket. I remembered about hurricane doors before the hail beat us unconscious. We found one on the south side, an airlock-type arrangement which could safely admit refugees. At that, I had hell's own time reclosing and dogging the outer door before we opened the inner.

We stumbled through, into a typical Sibyllan home. One room served for cooking, eating, sleeping, handcrafting, everything. Screens offered some pretense of privacy, but here they stood unused against the sooty, unornamented walls. A brick oven gave reasonable warmth, but the single lantern was guttering and demon-shaped shadows moved in every corner.

A man and his wife sat on a bench by a cradle that he must have made himself. She had her face against his breast, her arms around his neck, and wept, not loudly, only with a despair so complete that she had no strength left to curse God. He held her, murmuring, sometimes stroking her faded hair. With one foot he rocked the cradle.

They didn't notice us for a moment. Then he let her go and climbed erect, a burly man, his beard flecked with gray, his clothes clean but often patched. She remained seated, staring at us, trying to stop her tears and comprehend what we were.

Wind, rain, thunder invaded the stout walls. I heard the man say, slowly, 'You're from Earth.'

'Yes.' I introduced us. He shook hands in an absent-minded fashion and mumbled his own name too low for me to catch.

'You can stay here, sure,' he added. 'We got food in the cupboard till the storm passes. Afterward, Jimstown's walking distance.'

'We can do better than that,' I said, commanding a smile forth, trying to ignore our drowned-rat condition, for they needed whatever comfort was to be gotten. 'We have a car.'

Lauri went to the woman. 'Don't cry, please, my dear,' she murmured; somehow I heard her through the noise, and her head shone in the murk. 'I know your farm's wiped out. But you're leaving soon anyway, and we'll see you're taken care of, you and your whole fam – Oh!' She stopped. Her teeth gleamed, catching at her lip.

The woman was not pregnant. But, craning my neck, I too saw that the cradle stood empty.

'I buried her around sundown,' the man said, looking past me. His tone was flat and his face was stiff, but the scarred hands kept twisting together. 'A little girl. She lived several weeks. We hoped – And now the rain must've washed her out. I did think Sibylla might have let her sleep. We wrapped her up snug, and gave her a doll I'd made, so she wouldn't be too lonesome after we were gone. But everything's scattered now, I reckon.'

'I'm sorry,' I groped. 'Maybe . . . later – ' Barely in time, I saw Laurie's furious headshake. 'What a terrible thing.'

Laurie sat down by the wife and whispered to her.

Once, on our way home, she told me what had been confided that night, hoping it would influence my report. This was the one child they had had, after five miscarriages. The birth was difficult and the doctor did not think any more were possible.

I told her it was no surprise. Standing by that cradle, I had recalled the few children elsewhere and the many graves. And at once, like a blow to the guts, wildly swearing to myself I must be wrong, I saw the face of the alien enemy.

Jules d'Indre sat behind his desk, a shriveled, fussily dressed man whom it was wise to respect. He nodded, quick dip of bald head, as Brenner and I came in. 'Be seated, citizens,' he did not invite, he ordered.

I found the edge of a chair. My pulse thuttered and my palms were wet. Brenner leaned back, meeting those eyes, faintly smiling. 'How d'you do, sir?' he drawled.

'Let us not waste words,' d'Indre said. 'Perhaps you are not aware how uncommon a physical confrontation in line of business is on Earth. I would normally use a vidiphone three-way, and during working hours. Can you guess why I did otherwise?'

'Informality,' Brenner said. 'No record, no snoops, no commitments to anything. Suits me. We lived old-fashioned on Sibylla. Not that we wanted to, understand.' His smile departed, his voice grew crisp, I had a sense of sparks flying. 'It gave us some old-fashioned ideas, however, like about the rights of man.'

D'Indre's schoolmaster accent did not alter. 'Rights are forfeited when one perpetrates a felony.'

'Who's done what and with which unto whom?'

'The Colonial Fleet has been tied up on a useless mission for almost seventy years. Billions of munits have been spent.' D'Indre leaned forward. He tapped a pencil on the edge of the desk, *tick-tick* into an all-underlying silence. 'The first thing I wish to know, Brenner, is how many were privy to the hoax.'

The leather visage sought mine. 'What made you report the attack was faked?' Brenner asked calmly, even amiably.

'I didn't want to,' burst from me. 'I tried – everything – my whole team did. We couldn't risk Earth being unprepared, if there was any chance a hostile fleet existed. And – ' I noticed my hands reach toward him – 'we didn't want to hurt you!'

'I know,' he said, briefly serious. His tone lightened again: 'But I've got a curiosity. The fake was arranged by some mighty smart men. Time must've faded the evidence. What put you on?'

'Oh . . . any number of things,' I forced myself to say. 'Close study of certain pictures turned up some unlikely perspectives in them. Analysis of crater material gave results that were consistent with the explosion of stationary plants, not of warheads. Any warhead we could think of needs a fission trigger, or it'd be too bulky. Analyzing the bones of supposed missile victims, we got clear indications that they'd died years earlier. Some of the diaries and correspondence, allegedly from the immediate post-attack period, contradict each other more than is reasonable, when you apply symbolic logic. I could go on, but it's in the report. No single detail conclusive, but no doubt left after the whole jigsaw was fitted together.'

I wet my lips. 'Sir,' I said to d'Indre, 'our team discussed suppressing the facts. We decided we couldn't do that to Earth. But you should know we did seriously consider it. We were that sorry for these people.'

*Tick-tick.* 'You have not answered my question, Brenner.'

'Hey?' The Sibyllan coughed. 'How many were in on the conspiracy? Just a few. Key men that my dad recruited. Still fewer today. The least number necessary to keep things shuffled around so nobody who wasn't in on it would suspect.'

'That has to be true, sir,' I blurted. 'Ten thousand ordinary mortals can't keep a secret or act a role.'

'Obvious.' *Tick-tick.* 'How did you, or rather your predecessors, avoid massacring their own populace?'

'Well, everybody thanked his luck that he'd not been in a target area or was evacuated in time,' Brenner said. 'He heard about casualties, but they'd always happened somewhere else, in places where nobody lived that he knew. He couldn't check up, supposing it occurred to him. Sibylla never had global electronic communications, or fast transport except for some official flitters. What did exist – like a newspaper or three – was lost when the towns went. Took quite a spell even to re-establish a mail service. Meanwhile everything was confused, and refugees were getting relocated among strangers, and – The stunt wasn't easy, Dad told me. But it did come off. Later, histories and chronicles and such were written; and who had reason to suspect them? Everybody knew our numbers were way below the original forecasts, and dwindling. But accurate pre-disaster figures were filed only in certain heads now, that kept their mouths shut. And nobody had time to sit down and think hard. So it came to be taken for granted that the loss of people was mainly, if not entirely, due to the attack and its aftermath. I assure you, sir, nearly everyone among us honestly believes in the alien enemy.'

His gaze challenged d'Indre. 'Do what you like to me and my partners,' he said. 'We were ready for this, if the truth should come out. But you can't punish ten thousand who also got foxed!'

'Presumably the Director will not wish to do so,' d'Indre said as if stating a theorem. 'Nevertheless, the problem of assimilating them, so that they can make a living on this overcrowded world, may well prove insoluble. And individuals are apt to be subjected to mob violence. And it is politically impossible to send them to a different planet, when so many others desire that for themselves. Did the conspirators foresee this?'

'Yes,' Brenner said. He sat straight. The big fists clenched on his knees. 'But there was no mucking choice. We had to get off Sibylla. We – my father's group – didn't think Earth would fetch us just because we were slowly dying. We'd already gotten too many refusals of our pleas for help, only a little help. "Too expensive," we were told. "They cope with the same problems elsewhere. Why can't you?" Unquote.

'Expensive!' The word ripped from him, together with a detonating obscurity. I started where I sat. D'Indre did not change expression, but he stopped tapping that pencil. Brenner clamped lips together, took a breath, and went doggedly on: 'To be quite frank, sir, on the basis of what knowledge I have, I wouldn't put it past certain officials to fake incoming messages from a colony that stopped sending.'

For the first time, I saw d'Indre lose color. The pencil broke in his fingers. Doubtless Brenner noticed too, for he paused through several still seconds before he finished: 'Survival knows no law. My father and his men created a false enemy so their grandchildren could be saved from the real one.'

'Which was?' d'Indre whispered.

'Sibylla, of course,' Brenner said, almost as softly. 'The world where everything was wrong. Where the sum total defeated us. Like a woman who wouldn't miscarry *too* often in high gravity, except that she never got enough ultraviolet or oxygen, and did get too many hard roentgens, and had a poor diet, and was overworked, and the very daylight wasn't the right color for easy vision. . . . An entire world, fighting us on a hundred different fronts, never letting up. That was the alien enemy. We wouldn't have lasted another century.'

I said into the silence which followed: 'Earth has known some analogies. Like the Vikings, around the year 1000. They made themselves rulers of England, Ireland, Normandy, Russia. They ranged unbeatable through half of Europe. They settled Iceland, they discovered America. But they could not hold Greenland. They had a colony there, and it hung on for maybe four hundred years, always more isolated, poorer, smaller, hungrier, weaker. In the end it perished. When archaeologists dug up the skeletons of the last survivors, every one was dwarfed and deformed. Greenland had beaten them.'

'I've read about it,' Brenner said. 'Men won in the end. Eskimos, who had the right technology for the place. Europeans, later, with sheer power of machinery. We, our race, we'll lick Sibylla yet, one way or another. But it's taken the first battle. In such cases, a good general retreats.'

D'Indre had recovered his poise. 'I also know the history,' he said. 'Captain Simić's report was exhaustive. I wished, however, to add a personal encounter to my data store before deciding what disposal of this affair I should advise.'

Brenner folded his arms and waited.

'As a matter of fact,' d'Indre said, 'Captain Simić has already proposed a solution which seems viable to me. Parts of Earth remain empty because development has been economically unfeasible. The tropical deserts, for example, the Sahara or the Rub' al-Qali. Sand, stone, drought, low water table or none, fierce heat and light, no worthwhile minerals. Converting them by machine would tie up too much capital equipment and skilled personnel that are badly needed elsewhere. Theoretically, the task could be accomplished by minimal robotic and maximal hand labor. But who among the proles combines the necessary attitude and hardihood? It will be interesting to see if the Sibyllans do.'

Briefly, humanness broke through him. 'I am sorry, especially for the children,' he said. 'But under present circumstances, this is the best that anyone can give you.'

Brenner remained steady. 'I sort of expected it,' he said. 'The captain dropped a few hints on our way down here. What about us, uh, conspirators?'

D'Indre spread his hands. 'Your colony will need leadership. I daresay the Director will rule that providing such leadership is an accepted expiration.'

Brenner's own right hand crashed on the desk. Laughter roared from him. 'Why, man!' he cried. 'After what we've been up against, you think a nice kind Earthside desert's going to be any problem?'

Discussion dragged on. I took small part. My mind wandered and wondered. I didn't speak, lest I jeopardize the solution that was being hammered out. But take these people, I thought. A world battled them for generations. What those now alive had experienced was of no importance compared to what their germ plasm had experienced. With that natural selection in their past, what would they do with their future?

Ten thousand of them among billions – set down in the worst lands on Earth – could make a difference? Nonsense!

I got rid of the notion. I took command of my ship and went off on a voyage. I came home after eighty-five years and found that I had not thought nonsense after all.

# THE FAUN

A wyvern flew up in a thunder of splendid wings. A python tree coiled its branches. A chiming ran among the tiny red blossoms that covered the ground. Alien in the forest, a grove of pines stirred only to a breeze.

The boy, Tom, stepped out from among them. He was tall and slender, clad in a tunic of scaly leather, a knife at his belt, a rifle and packsack on his shoulders. Behind him came a cynopard, noiseless on six feet, fur shining the bluish green of the native leaves and spotted like flecks of the ruddy sunlight. They stood peering into shadowed thickets, listening to the many soft sounds and smelling the many pungent odors. Finally the boy nodded.

'Yes-s-s,' he said. 'Something is wrong. Yonder.'

He started off, quickly but warily. The cynopard paced him, its terrible head just beneath his left hand.

The man named Edmund Wylie floundered in the brush slightly out of breath, his gray beard and hair streaked with sweat.

*I will not panic; he told himself. I'm not lost. I've merely strayed from the others because beauty distracted me.*

He had seldom seen peacock moths before; they didn't survive captivity. Coming upon one in its home, he was bedazzled. All at once he realized why people here hung Japanese lanterns outdoors to attract the moths after dark, and made them a symbol of a developing style of life. He followed the radiant thing off the trail. When he turned to go back, all directions looked the same.

*I know I've blundered around, making matters worse,* he thought. *But my party certainly can't be more than a few kilometers off.*

That could be too much distance, though, in this wilderness. It could be effectively as far as the eleven light-years to Earth.

Foliage enclosed him and arched over him. Through its fronds he saw Epsilon Eridani. The sun disk showed twice as big as the Sol he dimly remembered from his childhood, and red-gold in a purple sky. He had always believed Arcadia lovely, an undespoiled planet waiting for man like a bride, more than worth decades in coldsleep aboard a spaceship, toil and danger of pioneering, isolation from the rest of humankind.

But he felt now, in his bones, that he belonged to city and machine. He did not quite understand the new generations, scattering themselves thinly across the world, speaking of co-operation with nature rather than war against it. These silences daunted him.

A shape streaked up one trunk and vanished among branches. Wylie caught a glimpse, and heard indignant chatter. A squirrel! *Why not? We settlers brought more than plant seeds. We took freeze-suspended embryos, every kind of animal, ready to grow to term in the gestation tanks as needed. The oddity is that the countryfolk aren't introducing terrestrial species faster.*

Reminded of past accomplishments, Wylie's mood brightened. He had not become what he was without self-confidence. Although middle-aged, he was in good physical condition. If no one found him, he could return on his own.

The party had flown to the cabin on Moonfish Lake. Finding it empty – the Faun apparently out on a mission – they hiked along a game trail for a look at the area. Thus Wylie didn't have the exact position of the hamlet he was visiting. However, if he traveled north he should at least reach open farmland in several hours.

Taking his bearings from the sun, he strode off. He was not aware of the thing that presently began to follow.

The boy halted again. Uneasiness bit into him. The cynopard winded it and bared teeth. Tom stroked the creature. 'Think I should try for an intuition?' he asked.

He often spoke to his animals. It was no eccentricity. At home, in school, anytime when he didn't range the woods, he acted as much as possible like an ordinary lad of thirty-four. (Or sixteen, if you were addressing an older person who thought in terms of the Earth calendar.) True, there were limits on his ordinariness. The natural gifts and the hard training that made him a Faun would always stand out – more and more, in fact, as the ecological project gained momentum. But otherwise he led a fairly normal life, which included the human habit of talking a lot.

'All I know is, some kind of trouble ahead,' he murmured. 'The birds are aloft and noisy, the mobile trees in defense posture, clues like that. Can we afford the time to get better information?'

The cynopard switched its tail. Tom made his decision, and opened himself to the forest.

The senses are keener than most of us suspect. The eye reacts to half a dozen quanta of light, the nose and tongue to a few parts per million, ears and skin to the merest ghosts of stimuli. And then individuals exist who can lower the threshold of perception at will. An ocean of visual detail, sounds, odors, tastes, vibrations, temperatures, thermal gradients, everything that there was to perceive, rolled over the Faun and engulfed him.

In that state, he did not use his conscious, reasoning mind. Yet his brain, his entire nervous system, was furiously active. No longer channeled in straight-line logic, it functioned like a multi-billion-cell analog computer. Primordial instinct and the wisdom of the body guided it. On a deeper level than thought, Tom comprehended his total environment.

'*You can't dispense with scientific method,*' Dr Krishnamurti had told him, Dr Nathu Krishnamurti, the young man who had helped create the new technique and was still perfecting it. '*Most of the time, you will carry biologist's equipment on your back, collect specimens, perform analyses, propose and test hypotheses, the usual procedures. They are necessary.*'

His eyes had kindled. '*But they are not enough, Tom,*' he said. '*That is why we want to train you and put you to work, even at your age. You have the rare inborn talent.*

'*We hope to make over this world until it is a paradise. But an ecology is too vast and complex for blind changes. Read the tapes from Earth. Read of rabbits in Australia, blights and beetles and dust bowls in America, continent-wide pollution and devastation.*

'*We have a new world here, a chance to begin afresh. Shall we make another mechanical desert, or shall we make it bloom? To help nature help us, we must trace out the myriad relationships in the web of life, their interactions, significance, value, meaning. That will be your career, Tom if you wish. You can find no higher calling.*'

The revelation faded. You couldn't take it for more than a few minutes in a row. But every time, you gained further insights, broader wisdom, to guide the ongoing research.

Tom didn't evaluate this experience. The fact he had been after was now too clear: *Not far hence, a city dweller wandered lost. And death was on his track.* He burst into a run.

The brush seemed to get in Wylie's way with malignant purpose. That wasn't true, he thought. The local inhabitants threaded an effortless way among such withes and tendrils. Cold comfort to him. Hot comfort, rather. His clothes were drenched with sweat. The breath went harshly in and out of his lungs. Better take a rest. A patch of open ground, shaded by a stand of redwoods that had already grown fifteen meters tall, invited him. As he sat down on a log, a native tree which the immigrants had overshadowed, he noticed he was trembling with weariness.

Confound this land! And the upcoming generation aimed to preserve its essential character?

Well, maybe they had a point. Although he was president of Arcadia's 10,000 people, Wylie knew he couldn't impose his will on history. He didn't want to, either. His responsibility was to guide the inheritors to a good start. That was why he'd flown here unannounced. To be sure, he also had a personal reason for wishing to surprise the Faun —

A steam-kettle hiss pierced his awareness. He sprang erect. His heart convulsed.

Three meters long, gorgeously iridescent, jaws agape and agleam with saber fangs, the dire lizard came out of the bushes and at him. He knew himself starkly for its meat. Those six legs could outrun, outclimb, outclaw the strongest man who ever lived. He snatched for his pocketknife, futile gesture, and stammered out the names of his wife and children.

The Faun appeared.

For an instant, Edmund Wylie's private world froze. He saw the length of the beast, aimed at him in mindless hunger and ferocity. He saw the boy like some kind of wood spirit, and the other beast at his heel, and the trees and glooms behind them. But everything focused on the rifle, the highpowered rifle on the boy's shoulder; and deliverance shouted within him.

Only . . . Tom didn't unsling the weapon. 'Get 'im!' he yelled, and plunged forward himself.

The cynopard sprang. It struck the dire lizard on the flank. Teeth ripped at scales. The lizard ululated eerily, swung around, whipped its tail with murderous force. The cynopard dodged but had to let go. It leaped in again, trying for the throat. Locked together, the two great animals rolled across the meadow.

They almost collided with Tom. He barely swerved aside. Wylie stood paralyzed by shock. Tom dragged at his arm. 'Get out of the way, sir,' he gasped. 'You could be killed.'

The pair of them found shelter in a thicket. The combat lasted only a few minutes. Evolution had not given the dire lizard an instinct of fear for men, but had instilled a healthy respect for the other big Arcadian carnivores. It disengaged and bolted into the underbrush. The cynopard yowled triumph and lolloped over to the Faun.

'Oh, you, you, you!' Tom hugged the huge form and buried his face in the fur. It was a little while before he stood up and confronted Wylie. 'You are okay, aren't you?'

'Y-yes,' the man said. He was a little faint, and his heart still fluttered. But he could think clearly again, and the habit of command was reviving in him. He leveled a hard glance at his rescuer. 'Except for one thing.'

'And neither got worse than some scratches and bites,' Tom said happily. Recollecting himself: 'Oh. I'm sorry. You were saying?'

'You could have taken that brute with your gun,' Wylie declared, word by word. 'I know what a shot you are. Instead, you risked both our lives. You – ' Briefly, he looked and felt old. His head shook. 'I don't understand you youngsters. I don't resonate with you any more. What has Arcadia done to you?'

Tom stood appalled. 'But I couldn't kill it!' he protested. 'Not when we'd every chance of saving you in a better way.' He steadied. 'I'm a Faun, sir. I've got a duty to the whole planet, to all the life on it.'

'Even dangerous life?'

'Nature needs predators. Dire lizards have grown too scarce as is. Among other things, they keep down the number of tricorns. Tricorns eat the bark of trees where peacock moths lay their eggs, and – ' Tom's voice faltered. He gripped the neck of his friend the cynopard, seeking consolation. 'I do so wish I could make you see it, sir. How man has to stop destroying and begin helping.'

Edmund Wylie regarded the boy for a long while. Piece by piece, his anger departed, and it was as if strength flowed into him instead. 'Maybe I do see,' he answered gently. 'Maybe I owe you thanks for more than just my life. Let's drop that "sir" nonsense, shall we?'

Tom's smile came awake. He seized the hands of the other. 'All right, Dad.'

# IN THE SHADOW

There was a man called Danilo Rouvaratz who signed the Petition of Rights. When it was denied and rioting became insurrection, he led the rebels in his own sector. A firegun killed him as the monitors entered Zagreb.

At that time the Gearch was Huang III, wily enough to understand the uses of mercy. He pardoned most of the insurgents, made certain reforms, and thus put out the fire. Still, he knew that embers remained under the ashes. Best would be to scatter them. Investigators learned that Danilo Rouvaratz had left several children. Government care was provided. Ten-year-old Karl went to a boarding school in North America, and thence to the Space Academy. He proved to be an excellent pilot, and his role in the hazardous rescue of the Mars liner *Flying World* made him quite a public hero. But he had always been a prickly, too independent sort, and his dossier suggested that some degree of resentment lingered in him. A very natural solution to the potential problem was to offer him a berth on the Acheron expedition. He ought to feel duly grateful for that; and he would most certainly be out of the way for a while.

Thus it was that he found himself nearing a star he could not see.

He did not know until too late. His boat was in orbit, under low reverse thrust, so that she spiraled in toward what he supposed was the burned-out dwarf he had come to find. He sat tense in his harness at the pilot board, eyes flickering from sky to radarscope to gauges which registered the emissions of test probes fired ahead. As soon as he got reflections from an astronomical body – and his instruments could pick out a meter-wide rock at a thousand kilometers – he would stop the jets and swing free. But the screens showed only random flickers, ghost images of atoms and electrons lost in vacuum.

Aaron Wheeler entered the control turret, balanced his slight deceleration-pressure weight against a handhold, and asked if there was any sign yet.

'No,' said Karl Rouvaratz. 'Get aft where you belong.'

Wheeler bridled. The movement was actually noticeable in his spacesuit. He was a lean, sharp-faced, gray-haired man of good family and considerable attainments. Throughout his life, people had deferred to him. 'May I remind you,' he snapped, 'that this trip is on my account? You are simply ferrying me to the object I am to study.'

Rouvaratz turned his blocky frame half around. His eyes flared green in the dark, rough countenance. 'While we're out here alone,' he said, 'I've got ship captain's authority. Go back. I'll let you know when we spot something. What do you think intercoms are for?'

Wheeler poised stiff and stubborn. Briefly, Rouvaratz wanted to force him. That would be easy and satisfying. The gods who gave the pilot two men's physical strength had put him in a milieu where he had no use for it. This was the basic source of his anger at the world.

But no. He must not leave his post while they were under power. And he must be diplomatic. The expedition comprised twenty human beings, almost a dozen astronomical units from home, receding fifty kilometers further with every second that passed. Mystery encompassed them, and if trouble came there could be no succor. If they did not work together, they were dead.

Darkness and knife-bright stars crowned Wheeler in the viewdome. Sol was cruelly radiant, but shrunken and strange. Acheron could not be found, not by any means save the fact of its monstrous pull. The boat fumbled through night.

Rouvaratz sighed. It was as if some of the weariness of the journey still possessed him, six months from Lunar orbit to the point where the *Shikari* intercepted her target. And then had followed tedious maneuverings; the firing of one radio rocket after another; the computation of where Acheron must be by the curvatures that were forced on their trajectories; the failure of telescopic search – all before this boat was sent to make a close approach. Nerves were thin.

*Firespit!* Rouvaratz thought. *Come off that. Doc O'Casey says we're in good shape.*

He spoke with care, his voice sounding hollow to him through the murmur of ventilators and air renewers, throb of thermonuclear powerplant, backpulse of the ion jets that splashed darkness with faint fire. 'Look, sir, we're closer in than I like, and still haven't seen a thing. Maybe some absorption effect is blocking our radar – but damn it, we should be able to see an occulting disc with the naked eye by now! When I do get an indication, we may turn out to be so near that I'll have to cut blast immediately. You could take a bad tumble, maybe even crash into the controls, gone null-gee without warning. For your own safety, please go strap in.'

'And for yours,' Wheeler gibed.

'Well, I enjoy being alive.'

'You don't act like it.'

Rouvaratz didn't bother to reply. He was habitually curt with his superiors. Even aboard the *Shikari,* he and the astrophysicist could hardly be said to move in the same social circles. A chance for privacy being as important as oxygen, on so long a cruise, cliques had inevitably formed within the gigantic hull. Wheeler did not roister and roughhouse with the engineer gang or party with the girls. Rouvaratz wondered what memories of Earth were dear to him. Surely not snowclad immensity on the Himalayas, or skipsailing in the salt wind across the Gulf of Mexico. (On a spaceship pilot's salary, you could afford the cost of entering what few outdoor preserves survived.) Most double surely not soarwing racing, or small oddball taverns in low-level Chicago Complex.

Studying him, Wheeler relented. 'Very well,' he said. 'Perhaps I misunderstood. I was never further out before than Luna Prime Observatory. You, though, don't realize – ' He broke off and left the turret.

Rouvaratz stayed. But the stars crowded in on him, brilliant and heartless as diamonds, unwinking as snake's eyes. He didn't know why they should appear strange to him. The constellations hadn't changed worth mentioning, in a mere billion and a half kilometers. Maybe the difference was that Sol had joined them, little more than the brightest of their horde. The things that were a man's real awareness – play of muscles under the skin, breath in the nostrils, a gust of air across the face, odors of machine oil and one's flesh – had lost their comfort.

He adjusted the spectroscope. Doppler shift in starlight gave a measure of velocity. So did the radio carrier wave from the distantly orbiting mother ship. A computer analyzed the data. Its screen declared that the boat was spinning furiously around the thing he could not detect.

He was startled to hear himself say into the intercom: 'Let's not fight, Professor. Could be I did speak too rough. What don't I realize?'

'Eh?' Rouvaratz could hear the astrophysicist's own astonishment, where he sat in his webbing among blank metal bulkheads. 'Oh. Yes. You don't know how important this is to me. I gave up much to join this expedition. And space is not kind to a middle-aged body. But for so rare and wonderful a phenomenon – ' A laugh, uncertain but nonetheless unexpected, cracked through his words. 'Why, I feel six years old again, on my birthday morning. Do you blame me for wanting to look at the gifts?'

Rouvaratz frowned, puzzled. Was a black dwarf that spectacular?

So they had told him. The Scientific Enterprise Board had long wanted to launch missions, telemetric probes at least, beyond the Solar System. But authorization was not forthcoming. Even the Gearchy must take taxpayers' opinions into account when planning something so expensive, whose rewards would be delayed for years and would never amount to more than pure knowledge. There was no hostile word spoken, however, when a journey was proposed to the thing called Acheron.

For it passed through the System, ripping Uranus into a wild new orbit, troubling mighty Jupiter, changing the galactic track of the sun itself. Earth was little perturbed, and the Lunar instruments swung eagerly in search: optical, radio, X-ray, particle detectors.

They got no whisper of response, not a photon, not an electron, not so much as an eclipse. The lure which drew the *Shikari* was, in the end, blackness and blankness.

Sometimes Rouvaratz wondered why the hell he had come along. The best rationale he could find was that after he got back, if he did, he would have prestige which he could use to propagandize for a real interstellar trip. Tau Ceti, say; that one must have planets, and you could coldsleep during the decades of the voyage. God, to walk on a world uncluttered by cities and crowds and governments and police, a world unraped by man! But the chance of finding New Earth in his lifetime was negligible. His reason didn't make sense. Maybe he only wanted to kick the cosmos in the teeth.

'Have you noticed something?' Wheeler exclaimed.

Rouvaratz started, then grinned. 'No. Sorry. I was woozing. Uh, I meant to ask why you're so excited. That is, I know this'll be the first body of its kind that has ever been observed. You might find some new law of nature. But aren't the odds against you? Doesn't theory pretty well predict what a star is like that's used up its last energy reserves?'

'Evidently not,' Wheeler said. 'It shouldn't be this . . . this invisible . . . unless it were a black hole – you know, a dead sun so compressed that light itself can't escape. And it hasn't enough mass to become one. Given a mass like Sol's, even in its extreme possible state of quantum degeneracy it should not be so small that we can't find it this close. Indeed, it probably shouldn't be dark at all; it ought to reflect rather brightly.'

His aloofness vanished. 'Pilot,' he said, 'if my hopes turn out to be justified, we will never see that star.'

'Huh?'

'You don't know? Didn't your briefings include – '

'Nothing. I'm just a slob of a jet jockey, remember? The scientists had no time to waste on me. Go on.'

'What we will see is a . . . a treasure of information . . . something unique in the galaxy, something to make me believe there really is a God who cares about us.'

'What's that?'

'Please.' Wheeler chuckled. 'Let me have my fun. I should be able to tell you before long if I am right or not.'

Rouvaratz clenched one big fist. 'I want to know what the devil we're getting into,' he said.

'If it's what I suspect, we can't possibly be hurt. If not, well, then I am as baffled as you. What is our current position?'

'Who knows, when we've got nothing to refer to except the computed centroid? But we're orbiting at 435 kilometers per second. If this were Sol, we'd be skimming the photosphere. We can't go much deeper into the gravitational well; wouldn't have enough reaction mass to get back out.'

'The pull is, then, increasing as if this were a sunlike body – right?'

'Uh-huh. And it shouldn't. If that's a neutron star, a chunk of collapsed matter smaller than Earth, its field ought to drop off so sharply that – '

Then they were struck.

This far into emptiness, there had seemed no reason to sacrifice other capabilities for the sake of keeping meteoroid spotters at maximum scope. Furthermore, evasive maneuvers are handicapped when one is hard by a powerfully attracting mass. Accordingly, the boat's automata were unable to react in time.

Rouvaratz's first sensation was shock. A troll's fist slammed him against his harness and rattled his head in the open helmet.

Fury toned through metal. Circuits arced over, the air smelled full of lightning. At once safety switches clashed open, the engines died, and the boat spun free. There was only the shriek of gases rushing out of the pierced hull.

'Close your faceplate!' he bawled automatically, and did so himself. His eardrums had almost burst as pressure dropped. But he had no chance to notice the pain, or be afraid, or do anything except whip through the motions of survival.

A glance across the instruments: most were functioning yet, he could see that the powerplant was undamaged, likewise the ion tubes. But one mass tank must have been cracked, letting liquid boil into space, for that indicator needle plummeted toward zero. Circuits printed in the vessel's structure registered damage sites. He threw off his harness and vaulted weightless from the seat.

Now the boat held vacuum. Light from the fluorescents, from sun and stars, fell in undiffused puddles, with death-black shadows around. Rouvaratz gave a shove and sped aft, clawing himself along by the handholds. In the main section, the sky glared at him through a hole punched in the plates. Wreckage trailed aft, out a broken bulkhead and thus to the tank from which the smasher had made its exit. Bits and pieces floated wherever he looked, chaos unleashed in an elemental silence. He looked upon the ruined air renewer and wanted to vomit.

A spacesuited figure moved awkwardly in his direction. 'Go away!' Rouvaratz yelled, with obscenities. Wheeler made scarecrow gestures. Rouvaratz realized his radio was off. He switched it on and said between clenched jaws: 'Get out of my God-damned way. You've killed us both, but I won't let you interfere with my job.'

'But – but what – ' Sunlight sickled past the gap in the side, casting Wheeler's face into ghastly highlights. 'What's happened?'

Rouvaratz snarled, grabbed him, and hustled him to the berth cabin. 'Strap in,' he ordered. 'Sit till I send for you.'

The other man flinched from him. He heard a near whimper, grunted, and returned to the main section.

In the hour or two that followed, he worked some of the wrath out of himself. He must catch loose material, and make a general inspection, and weld on repair plates, and test everything, and finally release air from the reserve stock – a considerable task for a single man, with skill and coolness prerequisite.

He didn't hurry. The boat circled in a balance of forces that could prevail till the galaxy burned out. It was sheer, incredible bad luck that she had been hit, in so vast a volume of space. The odds against another strike were literally astronomical.

All it took, though, was one, he thought.

After he had raised the mother ship on the maser and reported, he could do little. So, in the end, he summoned Wheeler to the control turret. They might as well try to figure out what had doomed them.

Alarm bells rang. Crewfolk hastened to their posts. Messages stabbed forth, notifying those boats which had gone to investigate other regions around Acheron. The *Shikari* reassembled her two sections and got underway.

She moved with care. The hull which had crossed space at a hundred kilometers per second was an enormous bubble, more frail than any of the auxiliary vessels she bore. Her approach to the dark star, matching velocities and assuming orbit, had been as cautious a maneuver as anyone ever carried out.

The strain had eaten at Commander Nathans, even before word came of disaster. He felt very old, looking forth into the glittery dark. *You've taken two good men,* he thought. *You want the rest of us also, don't you?*

Janice Falconet had no duties at the moment. Everyone must be a trained technician, but her assignment was to maintain the scientific instruments. Now she could merely sit in her cabin, enclosed by vibrating metal, and try not to weep. She failed.

Maura O'Casey, the biomed, had joined her, sensing that the girl needed company. 'Don't feel so badly, dear,' she murmured, and let the blond head rest on her shoulder. 'We aren't beaten yet. We'll get them back.'

'We have to!' Janice cried.

'Now – ' Maura checked herself. This was not the time to remind the other that casualties might well be expected. The cold and hollowness of space, blind brutality of matter with no friction or gravity to control it, cataracting radiation, that unseeable thing which had trapped the boat . . . Suddenly she understood that Janice's anguish was not from terror.

'You mean this is personal,' she said.

'W-w-well, our friends, we've got to be friends out here, we're all alone – ' Janice straightened and knuckled her eyes, hard.

'I doubt if Dr Wheeler would affect you so,' Maura said.

Janice stared. A shiver passed through her.

'Did you sign on because of Karl Rouvaratz?'

Maura got no reply except for the quick, ragged breathing. 'Doesn't matter, really,' she sighed. 'Same result if the attachment developed on board. You mustn't let it become too deep, you know.'

'Why not?' the girl defied her.

'You know perfectly well why not. The situation was explained to you over and over before we left. Our margin of survival is too slim as is, without letting in emotional rivalries, jealousies, intrigues, or even grief at someone's death. Keeping temporary company is fine. Exclusive relationships are not.' For a moment, Maura sounded wistful. 'I've passed beyond that. Perhaps I've forgotten how it feels to be young.'

Janice looked at her hands, twisted together in her lap, before answering. 'I'm sorry,' she said low. 'I do have some daydreams about after we get home.'

'Did – does Karl share them?'

'I don't know. He isn't the kind to, to reveal himself. He'll talk and joke about anyone else, most of the time. But he gets these silent moods. And he never says anything meaningful.'

'Meaningful to a woman, that is.' Maura smiled. 'Well, we're going to be with Acheron for at least a year, and then it's a long haul back. That's ample opportunity to work on a man, *provided* you observe the social articles of the expedition meanwhile.'

'I will,' Janice said forlornly. The implication penetrated. She tautened. 'What do you mean by "at least a year"?'

'We could stay indefinitely. The ship is a closed ecological system. If we come on something interesting – '

'I won't! They can't! We contracted for one certain period. To grow old out here – '

'One step at a time, child,' Maura counseled. 'First we have to save those men.'

*If we can,* her mind added. *I don't see how.*

Around and around the spaceboat hurtled, in a circle of nearly four and a half million kilometers' circumference. Chill enfolded her, wan sunlight fell on her flanks, the Milky Way rimmed her visual universe. Within the control turret, silence stretched like a drumhead over the little sounds of machinery and life. Rouvaratz could not grasp the thought that he fell through incandescence.

Storms raved, flames sheeted, light and heat flooded from that multi-billion year violence which is a star. He could not survive a fractional second. Nothing could. Yet his gauges showed vacuum outside, ordinary cosmic radiation, a weak plasma-borne magnetic field. His radio receiver hummed with the beam from the *Shikari*, rustled with spatial interference, the voice of nebulae and galaxies.

'I don't get you,' he said. A part of him wondered if he was deliberately being commonplace, downright stupid: one way to assert humanness. He regarded Wheeler. The astrophysicist was in the emergency co-pilot's seat by him. They could have talked over the intercom, but they needed each other's presence. 'Give me some detail about this theory of yours.'

'First, suppose you explain what our trouble is,' Wheeler retorted. His arrogance drew no anger now, it was so plainly a defense. He was chalk-white and a tic had developed in one eye-lid.

'A probe rocket hit us,' Rouvaratz said. 'One of the first that we shot off, from the mother ship as we came into range. The batteries ran down and it wasn't emitting any longer. You recall some probes were telesteered into close orbits around the computed centroid, to see how they'd behave and so give the math boys a line on what Acheron is like.'

'Kindly don't patronize me!' Wheeler paused and gulped. 'No, I'm sorry. My nerves are on edge. Tell me in any way you like.'

'Well, before the transmissions stopped, the orbits of the rocket shells had been figured out. Highly eccentric, for some reason, but we used an approach curve that ought not to have brought us anywhere near one of 'em. Only somehow, somebody was mistaken. I think I see why.'

'Me too.' Wheeler nodded, jerkily. 'The predictions of where the rockets would be were made on the assumption that Acheron is a neutron star, small and ultra-dense. Since the case is other-wise – yes, rapid precession; and the force-field itself varies un-predictably, according to variations in density within the star. I should have – No. Since the paths were, as I say, unpredictable, you and I would have had to accept the risk anyway.'

Rouvaratz choked. He came near hitting the older man. 'That's not so!' he rasped. 'If you brain-rotted snobs had told me what Acheron maybe was, I could've guessed at the danger and taken precautions – Argh!' He couldn't go on.

Wheeler sat quiet until the pilot seemed calmer. Then the astrophysicist said, as dryly as might be, 'If you think you are entitled to an apology, please accept mine. But no one intended to slight you. They simply didn't think you would be interested in what, remember, all the specialists but me considered a most remote possibility.'

Rouvaratz said nothing. Wheeler grimaced and went on: 'It's true, the data from the probes did not accord with Acheron being an ultra-dense ball. But there is good reason to think neutron stars may have extensive atmospheres. That would account equally well for the behavior of the rockets – and, indeed, would make them crash on the central globe before this boat arrived.

'The only solid evidence I had for my belief was that we failed to locate the star optically. And this could be explained, under some rather forced assumptions, by the light-bending properties of – '

Rouvaratz decided to be mollified before he was talked to death. 'Okay,' he interrupted, 'maybe you domebrains weren't being stupid. Maybe nature just took you by surprise. But in any case, you and me are in a box. We can spend what mass we've got left to recede quite a ways from Acheron. But we can't make rendezvous with *Shikari* or any other boat. They can't get near enough. This was the only craft with so much velocity-change capability that she could duck this far down into the star's gravity well and climb back up.'

'But can they not send us extra mass – oh, say aboard an unmanned auxiliary?'

'Huh! You don't know what it takes to lay alongside an object like that, under these kind of velocities.' Rouvaratz shrugged. 'We can try, of course. We plan to. But I have my doubts if we'll succeed. And we won't get more than one or two tries, you understand. Our air renewer is smashed beyond fixing with anything we have aboard. We've got a few days' worth of oxy in reserve. After that, good-bye, chum.'

Wheeler bit his lip.

'We're not in any rush at the moment,' Rouvaratz said. 'The *Shikari* – all the boats – will take a while to reach this neighborhood. So we wouldn't gain anything by starting our outward spiral for some hours yet. Before we commit ourselves to that . . . well, maybe we can think of a better way. Go on, man. Explain yourself. What the devil is this shadow matter of yours?'

Wheeler sniffed. 'I don't see how a supposedly educated man has failed to hear about one of the most basic items in physics.'

'Damn you,' Rouvaratz growled, 'I don't see how anybody can call himself educated who doesn't know diddly-squat about how the machine he's riding in works.' With an effort, he smoothed his tone. 'Could be the idea was mentioned in one of my classes, but not emphasized, so I forgot. We both had too much to learn, you and me, in our different specialties. Besides, the Gearchy doesn't encourage really liberal education. That might start people thinking.'

As expected, Wheeler was shocked out of his pique. Rouvaratz laughed with scant humor. 'Never mind. I always was a malcontent. Go on, Professor. If I've caught your drift, there's supposed to be another universe besides our own. The shadow universe, you call it? How can it be?'

'The idea was first advanced in the . . . the twentieth century, I believe, to account for certain anomalies,' Wheeler said. Talking, he gradually lost himself, until he was a lecturer and almost happy. 'You see, the long-lived component of the neutral K meson beam was found apparently to exhibit the two-pion decay mode, which would have violated the principle of CP invariance. That principle was so important that several attempts were made to construct a theory which would preserve it while explaining the data. The one which succeeded was the one which postulated the shadow universe. In fact, the hypothesis proved so fruitful that at last, in a modified and more elaborate form, it was incorporated into the body of fundamental physics. Of course, hitherto it was useful for nothing except theoretical calculations, so I must conclude it is not too surprising that you are not familiar with the concept.

'To continue. You have another universe of matter and energy, occupying the same space-time as ours and not dissimilar. But there is no strong interaction between the particles of these two universes. Thus we cannot detect shadow matter, or even shadow photons; they do not act upon our electromagnetic fields, or we on theirs.

'Weak interactions are not forbidden, however. This includes the K meson decay for which the theory was first advanced. There is a certain probability of a $K_1$ meson yielding two shadow pions, which then become undetectable by us.

'And, to be sure, gravitation is a weak force.'

*Like hell!* Rouvaratz thought. *What it's doing to this boat . . . But no. The whole mass of a star can't yank us to 500 KPS. Though that'll do to kill us.*

He shook himself a little, for the idea was an eerie one, and asked, 'How come we can't spot pions from the other universe's K mesons?'

'Oh, we could, given sufficient concentration,' Wheeler replied. 'Within Acheron, for example. Do you realize now why I was so excited? When it passed through the System, already then I dared hope it might really be a shadow sun. The possibility was discounted by everyone else, which I suppose is the reason it was never mentioned in the news accounts. But as we began to gather data, I grew more and more convinced. That's why I insisted on being the man to come with you.

'A shadow sun!' He spoke as Lancelot might have spoken of the Grail, and tears stood in his eyes. 'A thing we can probe, even enter ourselves with a specially built ship. We can trace out density gradients and their time variations, infer details of nuclear reactions, learn what men had resigned themselves to never learning. Quite probably our discoveries will revolutionize the whole of physics. And high time, too. They've gotten smug and stagnant on Earth, they think everything is known and nothing is left to do but add the next decimal point. If we could find another race on another planet, comparable to us but with a new outlook, a new knowledge and philosophy – ' His tone sank. 'But too few people are willing to make such an effort. The shadow star might perhaps serve as well.'

*Satan on a rocket!* Rouvaratz thought in surprise. *The old bastard is human after all. He's damn near likeable.*

He brought himself back to questions. 'I guess what we'd observe would be two pions appearing out of nowhere,' he said. Wheeler agreed. 'Then why haven't we ever done so?'

'Because the concentration of shadow matter in the region of Sol is too small,' the scientist explained. 'The chance of such an event is infinitesimal. That's quite plausible, of course. Space is mostly empty. No doubt we lie somewhere between galaxies, as far as the shadow universe is concerned.

'The theory has had great cosmological value. The existence of two complexes makes the interstellar medium twice as dense as it would otherwise be, gravitationally speaking. That helps account for the observed distribution of our own galaxies. But still, this is a fantastically lucky accident, that we have found this actual sample.'

'Luck? Huh!' Rouvaratz managed a grin. 'Well, I suppose you could say so. How'd it happen, do you think?'

'I daresay Acheron escaped from its home galaxy. The speed suggests as much.'

'Planets?'

'Why not? We can find them by their gravitational effects.'

Wheeler returned to immediate reality. 'But I admit our first aim must be to escape. Are you quite certain that our prospect of matching up with a reaction mass carrier is poor?'

'I am,' Rouvaratz said. His flicker of philosophical interest died out.

'Ah . . . what about some less conventional procedure? Don't forget, this is an unconventional situation. You may be so used to thinking in terms of ordinary astronautics that – '

'Shut up!' Rouvaratz exploded.

He clamped his fists together. Rage mounted anew, driving out all else. He could stand dying – but for some better reason than a stupid failure of communication between men from two social orders. And in some better way than suffocation, the husk of him rattling forever around this phantom of a sun. *Let me go like my father,* he thought, *in battle, with something real to hold on to and fight with. Let me charge my enemy head on.*

Charge!

An oath tore from him. Wheeler asked what he meant. Rouvaratz ignored the question, scarcely heard. His lips moved with unspoken calculation and he stared out at the stars like a blind man.

Then he cracked down the maser switch and barked, 'Hello, *Shikari.* Me here. Get me Navigator Chai, and have him make ready to do some high powered figuring.'

Waiting was the hardest part. Commander Nathans grew yet more shriveled and gray while the time passed. Silence filled the bridge, the whole interior of the ship. Those who were aboard stared at each other, and away again, and fumbled with things. Janice Falconet sat hard by Maura O'Casey, but a shadow wall had risen around her and words or gestures did not seem to penetrate.

Sweat runneled from Chai and his gang where they hunched over their instruments. No telescope they had would reveal what was happening, at the distance which the mother ship must keep. Radar had lost the boat and could not find her; likewise the communications beam. Nothing but the radiation of her jets tracked her as she plunged into Acheron.

*Into:* down toward the core of the sun, where pressures reached the millions of atmospheres, temperatures the millions of degrees, where atoms were stripped bare and flung together with such ferocity that they fused and burned. Yet to men, those were ghosts, untouchable, unreal. Reality was the roar and shudder of thrust, barbarous acceleration, the grip of a mass as great as Sol's.

One could imagine: Rouvaratz among the thunders, eyes locked to instruments, fingers slugging across controls, sweat rivering over his own skin, his weight become nearly too huge a burden to bear. Yet he must drive, with nigh absolute precision, through shifting vectors that had been calculated for him – knowing the whole while that the computation was based on a handful of data, a hatful of theory, and might be altogether wrong.

One could imagine: Wheeler in his couch, frail frame dragged down into itself till bones creaked and heartbeat stuttered, maybe fainted, maybe dead.

One could imagine: the boat spouting flame across heaven, then running for some minutes inert, reeled in by the shadow sun, until time came to swing onto a new line and leap once more under power.

Inward – around the star's core – then the ultimate acceleration, everything the jets could give, everything the pilot could endure.

For the energy of reaction mass is not only kinetic. It has a potential component, due to its position in some given gravity field. Had the boat followed normal procedure and spiraled out, none of the potential would have been realized. Indeed, kinetic energy would have been spent simply to raise unexhausted mass higher.

Falling, the boat was flung in a cometary path around the centroid of Acheron. At the moment when her direction was reversed and she headed back out, she made her great effort; all else had just been to steer her into that orbit. Rather than being carried up again, her reaction mass was left behind, near the bottom of the gravity well, where it could supply the maximum energy.

The principle is simple. Oberth himself first noticed it, when space flight lived nowhere but in the dreams of a few. It is, in fact, routinely used in plotting departure maneuvers from the vicinity of a planet. Rouvaratz had not thought of it at once because he, like every pilot, was conditioned to stay well clear of the sun. Suns eat people.

Acheron did not. None of its blaze could touch a man. But of course the computation had been difficult. The boat was not to swing around a point mass, but to go through a stellar object of varying density. The law of attraction was no longer New-

104

ton's familiar inverse-square rule; it had trigonometric factors. And too many parameters could only be guessed at.

On the mother ship, on every boat, they waited.

*'Here they come! I've got them!'* The animal part of the radarman screamed the words. His hands danced over the knobs with a life of their own. Numbers poured forth, were analyzed in seconds, told Navigator Chai what was happening.

Breath gusted from his lungs. 'They made it,' he said. 'They've got more than escape velocity. Much more.'

He vanished into mathematics. When he emerged, he knew how the boat was orbiting and which auxiliary could best make rendezvous when she was far enough out. Commands raced over the maser.

No token came from Rouvaratz. Perhaps he was dead. Even with modern anti-acceleration drugs, no one should have had to take such pressure. Perhaps weight had broken some part of his communications system. In any event, time must pass before the other boat could join him. Once more men had to wait.

And wait.

Until the speaker croaked: 'Rouvaratz to *Shikari*. I think I've centered you. Do you read me?'

'Yes, yes, yes! How are you?'

More waiting, while photons crossed space and back again.

'Operational, I think.'

'Wheeler?'

'I don't know. I just came back to consciousness myself, and he's not very strong. No response from him. I'm about to go have a look.' The breath whistled through Rouvaratz's teeth. 'Stars out yonder,' he mumbled. 'Hello, universe.'

Maura O'Casey released him from sickbay after twenty-four hours. It felt good to have weight underfoot; the *Shikari* was spiraling out of Acheron's presence at a steady one gee. Prolonged free fall was not simply bad for you physically, however much counteracting pharmacopoeia you loaded yourself with, he thought. Some kind of insult as well – for him, at any rate. He wanted to use his muscles.

Now he'd get the chance. O'Casey didn't want him piloting till he was entirely recovered. The *Shikari* would assume a reasonable orbit, divide her sections, link them with five kilometers of whisker-wire cable, and go into a centrifuging spin.

He chuckled.

'What's so funny?' Janice asked. She held his arm closely, as they walked down the bare, thrumming corridor.

'A tag. The little star that isn't there.'

She shivered. 'Don't speak of that thing. It nearly killed you.'

'Well, it tried, but not quite hard enough. Even Wheeler should be back in commission after a week or two. Last time I looked in, he was giving Doc hell. Wants loose already, to start probing Acheron.'

Janice winced. 'How I wish it had been what we supposed. A cinder, not a ghost.'

'By its lights, we're the ghosts. More so. It probably has planets, and maybe one or two of the planets have life. In this universe, we're all the life there is from here to Sol.'

'I know, I know,' she whispered. 'I remember in my night-mares.'

'So we – Hoy!'

The intercom voice rolled down the passageways. Echoes gave an iron resonance, not entirely human. But the speaker was only little Commander Nathans.

'General announcement. General announcement. I, ah, I think everyone will be interested. A discovery has been made like – frankly, I have trouble believing it myself. Word has come in from Boat Four, pilot Krishnamurti and physicist Oliveira. You know that, er, as soon as the rescue was effected, what with the boats being in the region of the shadow sun anyway, we started them on a search for planets. Well, a planet has been found. It is of approximately Earth's mass, about one astronomical unit from the primary. The boat is now in surface orbit around it and, ah, certain tests which Dr Wheeler suggested are being prepared. Over.'

Rouvaratz stood still, then suddenly slapped his thigh with a pistol noise and shouted, 'How *about* that?'

'Yes, yes,' Janice said through tense lips. 'But –'

'Don't you get the point?' He grabbed her shoulders with bruising force. 'Earth-type planet around a Sol-type star. Almost bound to be life!'

'Specters,' she said in a shaken tone. 'We'll never know. One more thing to make us lie awake.'

'But maybe we will find out! I've been thinking. And Wheeler and I talked some while we waited to be picked up. If Acheron escaped from its home galaxy, well, that must've been one whale of a time ago. You don't cross a million or so light-years over-night. So the planet must be old. Older than Earth. It's had time

106

for intelligence to evolve and . . . and grow beyond us – Don't you see?'

She flushed with rebellion. 'No, I don't. That is, you may be right, but how can we ever tell?'

'Mesons. Any large nuclear powerplants they have must be grinding out so many K mesons on the side that we can spot the pions that get formed in our own universe. If we do, then we can rig a beam generator of our own. Get into the same orbit, right at the planetary center. Fire our beam so fast that we get the benefit of relativistic time contraction and it doesn't decay too far before it reaches the surface. Use a rotating system, so we always hit the same point. A point where we know there is a powerplant. Somebody ought to be on hand to detect and reply to us – '

'If, if, if!' she exclaimed, not far from tears. 'Go ahead and try. You won't get any answer out of your damned ghosts!'

They did.

Ten men and ten women filled the common room of the *Shikari*. The artists among them had attempted to brighten the place with murals, but somehow those wistful landscapes only underlined a starkness. The sounds of breath, muttered conversation, shuffled feet and chairs slid back, like the endless hum of the ship herself, flickered above immortal silence.

Commander Nathans rose and faced them. He had driven this vessel across desolation, and he could still drive her home. But the years had gnawed him, until he could no longer direct his people against their wills. Small, stooped, faintly trembling, he said:

'You: ah, you know why we are met. But I think best that, ah, the issue be summarized. Otherwise, well, we might waste valuable time talking at cross purposes.

'There is life on Shadow Earth. Intelligent life, with a technology at least equal to ours and probably superior. We know this because our meson-pion bursts produced a very quick response, a corresponding set of bursts aimed directly at the center of the planet where the boat was. This proves an instant comprehension of what, ah, what was going on. It also proves an ability to send a particle beam straight through their world. Whether they have a tunnel, or use some induction effect, or whatever, this is something man cannot do. And they must be eager to communicate.'

'I should think so!' Rouvaratz barked. 'Judus! Through their entire history, they've been in what they see as inter-galactic space. Not another star in sight, nothing but a few spiral wisps. I bet they took a million years to go from farming to science. They know they've passed by a sun they can't spot, and that's the whole of what they know. Those poor, lonely devils!'

'Please.' Nathans winced. 'Such things have been said very often in the past several watches. This is a business meeting.'

'But damnation, the business is emotional. We have to decide what we want to do.' Janice plucked at Rouvaratz's arm. He grumbled and subsided.

'The problem is this,' Nathans said. 'Pions offer a means of communication. We can go from a pulse code to . . . anything, theoretically. In time, we can even exchange pictures, for example by specifying points on a diagram. But that will take a great deal of time and effort. We will have to build a far more elaborate setup than, er, anything a boat can carry. In fact, we shall have to establish the *Shikari* within Shadow Earth and make our research center there. Then we must experiment, and develop our equipment, and commence the slow process of constructing a mutual language. The project will require years just to start. Centuries will not exhaust it, I am sure. But you are enlisted for a one-year stay. Ah . . . under the articles of the expedition, barring emergencies, a two-thirds majority is required to modify those articles. Thereafter the minority is bound by them.

'In short, we must vote whether to remain or return. The floor is now open to discussion.'

Hands flew high. 'Dr Wheeler?' Nathans said.

The astrophysicist rose. Zeal flamed from him. 'Everybody knows my wishes,' he said. 'A year – no, less – hardly suffices to begin studying Acheron. I would gladly give the rest of my life to that. But of course you aren't all my colleagues. So I would like to remind you what Shadow Earth can mean. A whole world – a geology, meteorology, oceanography, chemistry, biology – an entire civilization, with its own long experience, its arts and philosophies – yes, its science, too. Conceivably, fantastic thought but perhaps, they can give us a method to travel faster than light. Thus the whole galaxy would be opened to mankind. But quite without any such result, what we can tell Earth will be like nothing Earth has imagined. We must stay. It is our duty.'

'Chief Montelius? I gather you are in opposition.'

'I am,' said the boss engineer. 'I've got kinfolk at home. If Earth wants to know more about the shadow universe, they can send another expedition, manned by people who're willing to go. Me, I'll stay put.'

Janice halted a cheer.

'Ah . . . no, no, Dr Wheeler, please wait your next turn . . . Dr Settle?'

'I'm not sure that Earth would send another ship,' said the plasma dynamics man. 'I'll speak frankly and trust that no one will repeat my remarks if we do return. The decision would lie with the Gearch. And he will probably think twice. A scientific and philosophical revolution would bring a social revolution. He needn't flatly refuse. It would do to maintain that, since Acheron is after all getting farther away, the notion is unfeasible.'

Rouvaratz sprang to his feet. 'That's right!' he shouted.

'You're out of order,' Nathans protested.

'Sorry. But listen.' The big form loomed over the assembly, half wrathful, half pleading. 'When did a government that has to gun down its own people ever want something really new? It was okay to give the scientists their toys. An expedition to some useless dead star kept them happy, and also kept them away from human affairs where they might've gotten interested in things like freedom. But this? No! I've been there, I tell you.

'If we stay, and beam back what we learn, they won't have any choice but to send another ship with more equipment. The Gearchy depends on the technician class to keep the world running. Get those boys interested – and once we start sending home some real information, they will be – the government'll have to give in and hope for the best. Then you can go home, if you want.'

'We're receding every second,' Janice wailed. 'The new ship would have to be built – and get here – How many years?'

Chaos broke loose. Everyone was up, clamoring into his neighbor's mouth. Nathans spoke and was not heard.

Rouvaratz jumped to the front of the room. He filled his lungs and bellowed across the tumult. '*Quiet!* Pipe down or I'll start breaking some heads!'

'Go on and try,' Montelius said, red-faced.

Rouvaratz looked at him, from a greater height and from his own youth, before saying with a gentleness that sliced through the dying racket: 'You're my friend, Conrad, and I'd sure hate to get rough with you. But I can, and you know it.'

'Karl,' Janice pleaded. The sound reached his ears but not his brain.

He roared them to order and then funneled all the vitality

there was in him into his words and his presence.

'Look,' he said. 'You want to leave, some of you. Go back to the green hills of Earth. What green hills? If you're rich, you can find a square kilometer here and there not cluttered by some stinking human warren. If you're willing to do as the state tells you, you can live nice and peaceful, like an ox in a stall. But I don't think you're that kind. You wouldn't have come in the first place if you were.

'We won't have a bad life where we are. We've got room aboard ship. If we disassemble the drive units, we can have twice as much room. Those who want can redecorate the place. Good Lord, didn't the old-time monks get along on less?

'And we won't be sitting around bored, either. Those fellows on Shadow Earth are smart. I'll bet you googolplex plutons that they'll find a way to establish meaningful talk with us inside a year or two. As we start to learn what they know, why, we'll be building apparatus and conducting experiments till hell wouldn't have us. Okay, maybe ship number two won't arrive soon. But we'll not be old when she does. Me, I'd like to stick around afterward, too. Unless we've gotten us a Shadow Earth type boat which'll take us around the galaxy. Have we any right to deny our race a chance like that? Or the million other chances that we really can be sure will come?

'But never mind. I'm no damn altruist myself. I only say we can have fun here – more fun than any men or women have had since Columbus took off. How about that?'

There is a mystery and magic in power. Call it band-wagon psychology, call it charisma, call it *mana*: you have still merely tacked a name to what you don't understand. Nathans had given his away, to this ship and to those he had commanded before her. Wheeler had never had any. But in today's confrontation, Karl Rouvaratz was physically the strongest creature aboard. That shouldn't have mattered; a fight was out of the question. However, in some jungle fashion it did matter. And he was stronger yet in his psyche, for he knew exactly what he wanted.

He made enough of them want it too.

Afterward, when they were alone in his cabin, Janice regarded him for a long while. She did not cry. Despair was behind her.

'I guess I should apologize,' he said uncomfortably. 'To you, anyway.'

'No need.' Her words fell flat into the mechanical murmur around them.

'I know you'd rather go home and raise kids and – '

'Not you, though.' She attempted a smile. 'So I'd better change my mind.'

After a pause, she went on, 'But I can't help wondering. Why do you want to stay . . . here, locked in metal for the rest of your life, with nothing around you but unreachable stars? You're no scientist yourself. You won't be talking to Shadow Earth.'

'Someday I will,' he said. 'With my opposite number, a space pilot in their universe.'

'Oh, yes, you have your Quixote dream of a galactic drive. But the hope is so tiny. You must admit that; you're no fool. And as for everything else, the science, the engineering, the fresh new outlook if it isn't too alien for us – even what changes might happen on Earth – those are sort of religious goals, and you're not a very religious man. Why, Karl? Revenge?'

'I don't think so.' He sat down on the bunk beside her.

'What, then?'

'Something I have this minute, right in my hand.' His gaze left her, went to the bulkhead and saw visions beyond, Polaris, Andromeda, the whole sister cosmos. 'Freedom. I'm my own man now.'

# TIME LAG

*522 Anno Coloniae Conditae:*

Elva was on her way back, within sight of home, when the raid came.

For nineteen thirty-hour days, riding in high forests where sunlight slanted through leaves, across ridges where grass and the first red lampflowers rippled under springtime winds, sleeping by night beneath the sky or in the hut of some woodsdweller – once, even, in a nest of Alfavala, where the wild little folk twittered in the dark and their eyes glowed at her – she had been gone. Her original departure was reluctant. Her husband of two years, her child of one, the lake and fields and chimney smoke at dusk which were now hers also, these were still too marvelous to leave.

But the Freeholder of Tervola had duties as well as rights. Once each season, he or his representative must ride circuit. Up into the mountains, through woods and deep dales, across the Lakeland as far as The Troll and then following the Swiftsmoke River south again, the route ran which Karlavi's fathers had traveled for nearly two centuries. Whether on hailu back in spring, summer, through the scarlet and gold of fall, or by motorsled when snow had covered all trails, the Freeholder went out into his lands. Isolated farm clans, forest rangers on patrol duty, hunters and trappers and timber cruisers, brought their disputes to him as magistrate, their troubles to him as leader. Even the flitting Alfavala had learned to wait by the path, the sick and injured trusting he could heal them, those with more complex problems struggling to put them into human words.

This year, however, Karlavi and his bailiffs were much preoccupied with a new dam across the Oulu. The old one had broken last spring, after a winter of unusually heavy snowfall, and 2000 hectares of bottom land were drowned. The engineers at Yuvaskula, the only city on Vaynamo, had developed a new construction process well adapted to such situations. Karlavi wanted to use this.

'But blast it all,' he said, 'I'll need every skilled man I have, including myself. The job has got to be finished before the ground dries, so the ferroplast can bond with the soil. And you know what the labor shortage is like around here.'

'Who will ride circuit, then?' asked Elva.

'That's what I don't know.' Karlavi ran a hand through his straight brown hair. He was a typical Vaynamoan, tall, light-complexioned, with high cheekbones and oblique blue eyes. He wore the working clothes usual to the Tervola district, leather breeches, mukluks, a mackinaw in the tartan of his family. There was nothing romantic about his appearance. Nevertheless, Elva's heart turned over when he looked at her. Even after two years.

He got out his pipe and tamped it with nervous motions. 'Somebody must,' he said. 'Somebody with enough technical education to use a medikit and discuss people's difficulties intelligently. And with authority. We're more tradition-minded hereabouts than they are at Ruuyalka, dear. Our people wouldn't accept the judgment of just anyone. How could a servant or tenant dare settle an argument between two pioneers? It must be me, or a bailiff, or – ' His voice trailed off.

Elva caught the implication. 'No!' she exclaimed. 'I can't! I mean . . . that is – '

'You're my wife,' said Karlavi slowly. 'That alone gives you the right, by well-established custom. Especially since you're the daughter of the Magnate of Ruuyalka. Almost equivalent to me in prestige, even if you do come from the other end of the continent, where they're fishers and marine farmers instead of woodsfolk.' His grin flashed. 'I doubt if you've yet learned what awful snobs the free yeomen of Tervola are.'

'But Hauki, I can't leave him.'

'Hauki will be spoiled rotten in your absence, by an adoring nanny and a villageful of tenant wives. Otherwise he'll do fine.' Karlavi dismissed the thought of their son with a wry gesture. 'I'm the one who'll get lonesome. Abominably so.'

'Oh, darling,' said Elva, utterly melted.

A few days later she rode forth.

And it had been an experience to remember. The easy, rocking motion of the six-legged hailu, the mindless leisure of kilometer after kilometer – where the body, though, skin and muscle and blood and all ancient instinct, gained an aliveness such as she had never before felt – the silence of mountains with sunlit ice on their shoulders, then bird-song in the woods and a river brawling; the rough warm hospitality when she stayed overnight with some pioneer, the eldritch welcome at the Alfa nest – she was now glad she had encountered those things, and she hoped to know them again, often.

There had been no danger. The last violence between humans on Vaynamo (apart from occasional fist fights, caused mostly by sheer exuberance and rarely doing any harm) lay a hundred years in the past. As for storms, landslides, flood, wild animals, she had the unobtrusive attendance of Huiva and a dozen other 'tame' Alfavala. Even these, the intellectual pick of their species, who had chosen to serve man in a doglike fashion rather than keep to the forests, could only speak a few words and handle the simplest tools. But their long ears, flat nostrils, feathery antennae, every fine green hair on every small body, were always aquiver. This was their planet, they had evolved here, and they were more animal than rational beings. Their senses and reflexes kept her safer than an armored aircraft might.

All the same, the absence of Karlavi and Hauki grew sharper each day. When finally she came to the edge of cleared land, high on the slopes of Hornback Fell, and saw Tervola below, a blindness that stung descended momentarily on her eyes.

Huiva guided his hailu alongside her. He pointed down the mountain with his tail. 'Home,' he chattered. 'Food tonight. Snug bed.'

'Yes.' Elva blinked hard. *What sort of crybaby am I, anyhow?* she asked herself, half in anger. *I'm the Magnate's daughter and the Freeholder's wife, I have a University degree and a pistol-shooting medal, as a girl I sailed through hurricanes and skindove into grottos where fangfish laired, as a woman I brought a son into the world . . . I will not bawl!*

'Yes,' she said. 'Let's hurry.'

She thumped heels on the hailu's ribs and started downhill at a gallop. Her long yellow hair was braided, but a lock of it broke loose, fluttering behind her. Hoofs rang on stone. Ahead stretched grainfields and pastures, still wet from winter but their shy green deepening toward summer hues, on down to the great metallic sheet of Lake Rovaniemi and then across the valley to the opposite horizon, where the High Mikkela reared into a sky as tall and blue as itself. Down by the lake clustered the village, the dear red tile of roofs, the curve of a processing plant, a road lined with trees leading to the Freeholder's mansion. There, old handhewn timbers glowed with sun; the many windows flung the light dazzlingly back to her.

She was halfway down the slope when Huiva screamed. She had learned to react fast. Thinly scattered across all Vaynamo, men could easily die from the unforeseen. Reining in, Elva snatched loose the gun at her waist. 'What is it?'

Huiva cowered on his mount. One hand pointed skyward.

At first Elva could not understand. An aircraft descending above the lake . . . what was so odd about that? How else did Huiva expect the inhabitants of settlements hundreds of kilometers apart to visit each other? — And then she registered the shape. And then, realizing the distance, she knew the size of the thing.

It came down swiftly, quiet in its shimmer of drive fields, a cigar shape which gleamed. Elva holstered her pistol again and took forth her binoculars. Now she could see how the sleekness was interrupted with turrets and boat housings, cargo locks, viewports. An emblem was on the armored prow, a gauntleted hand grasping a planetary orb. Nothing she had ever heard of. But —

Her heart thumped, so loudly that she could almost not hear the Alfavala's squeals of terror. 'A spaceship,' she breathed. 'A spaceship, do you know that word? Like the ships my ancestors came in, long ago . . . Oh, bother! A big aircraft, Huiva. Come on!'

She whipped her hailu back into gallop. The first spaceship to arrive at Vaynamo in, in, how long? More than a hundred years. And it was landing here! At her own Tervola!

The vessel grounded just beyond the village. Its enormous mass settled deeply into the plowland. Housings opened and auxiliary aircraft darted forth, to hover and swoop. They were of a curious design, larger and blunter than the fliers built on Vaynamo. The people, running toward the marvel, surged back as hatches gaped, gangways extruded, armored cars beetled down to the ground.

Elva had not yet reached the village when the strangers opened fire.

There were no hostile ships, not even an orbital fortress. To depart, the seven craft from Chertkoi simply made rendezvous beyond the atmosphere, held a short gleeful conference by radio, and accelerated outward. Captain Bors Golyev, commanding the flotilla, stood on the bridge of the *Askol* and watched the others.

The light of the yellow sun lay incandescent on their flanks. Beyond reached blackness and the many stars.

His gaze wandered off among constellations which the parallax of fifteen light-years had not much altered. The galaxy was so big, he thought, so unimaginably enormous . . . Sedes Regis was an L scrawled across heaven. Tradition claimed Old Sol lay in that direction, a thousand parsecs away. But no one on Chertkoi was certain any longer. Golyev shrugged. Who cared?

'Gravitational field suitable for agoric drive, sir,' intoned the pilot.

Golyev looked in the sternward screen. The planet called Vaynamo had dwindled, but remained a vivid shield, barred with cloud and blazoned with continents, the overall color a cool blue-green. He thought of ocherous Chertkoi, and the other planets of its system, which were not even habitable. Vaynamo was the most beautiful color he had ever seen. The two small moons were also visible, like drops of liquid gold.

Automatically, his astronaut's eye checked the claims of the instruments. Was Vaynamo really far enough away for the ships to go safely into agoric? Not quite, he thought – no, wait, he'd forgotten that the planet had a five percent greater diameter than Chertkoi. 'Very good,' he said, and gave the necessary orders to his subordinate captains. A deep hum filled air and metal and bones. There was a momentary sense of falling, as the agoratron went into action. And then the stars began to change color and crawl weirdly across the visual field.

'All's well, sir,' said the pilot. The chief engineer confirmed it over the intercom.

'Very good,' repeated Golyev. He yawned and stretched elaborately. 'I'm tired! That was quite a little fight we had at that last village, and I've gotten no sleep since. I'll be in my cabin. Call me if anything seems amiss.'

'Yes, sir.' The pilot smothered a knowing leer.

Golyev walked down the corridor, his feet slamming its metal under internal pseudogravity. Once or twice he met a crewman and accepted a salute as casually as it was given. The men of the Interplanetary Corporation didn't need to stand on ceremony. They were tried spacemen and fighters, every one of them. If they chose to wear sloppy uniforms, to lounge about off duty cracking jokes or cracking a bottle, to treat their officers as friends rather than tyrants – so much the better. This wasn't the nice-nelly Surface Transport Corporation, or the spit-and-polish Chemical Synthesis Trust, but IP, explorer and con-

116

queror. The ship was clean and the guns were ready. What more did you want?

Pravoyats, the captain's batman, stood outside the cabin door. He nursed a scratched cheek and a black eye. One hand rested broodingly on his sidearm. 'Trouble?' inquired Golyev.

'Trouble ain't the word, sir.'

'You didn't hurt her, did you?' asked Golyev sharply.

'No, sir, I heard your orders all right. Never laid a finger on her in anger. But she sure did on me. Finally I wrassled her down and gave her a whiff of sleepy gas. She'd'a torn the cabin apart otherwise. She's prob'ly come out of it by now, but I'd rather not go in again to see, captain.'

Golyev laughed. He was a big man, looming over Pravoyats, who was no midget. Otherwise he was a normal patron-class Chertkoian, powerfully built, with comparatively short legs and strutting gait, his features dark, snubnosed, bearded, carrying more than his share of old scars. He wore a plain green tunic, pants tucked into soft boots, gun at hip, his only sign of rank a crimson star at his throat. 'I'll take care of all that from here on,' he said.

'Yes, sir.' Despite his wounds, the batman looked a shade envious. 'Uh, you want the prod? I tell you, she's a trouble-maker.'

'No.'

'Electric shocks don't leave any scars, captain.'

'I know. But on your way, Pravoyats,' Golyev opened the door, went through, and closed it behind him again.

The girl had been seated on his bunk. She stood up with a gasp. A looker, for certain. The Vaynamoan women generally seemed handsome; this one was beautiful, tall and slim, delicate face and straight nose lightly dusted with freckles. But her mouth was wide and strong, her skin suntanned, and she wore a coarse, colorful riding habit. Her exoticism was the most exciting thing: yellow hair, slant blue eyes, who'd ever heard of the like?

The tranquilizing after-effects of the gas – or else plain nervous exhaustion – kept her from attacking him. She backed against the wall and shivered. Her misery touched Golyev a little. He'd seen unhappiness elsewhere, on Imfan and Novagal and Chertkoi itself, and hadn't been bothered thereby. People who were too weak to defend themselves must expect to be made booty of. It was different, though, when someone as good-looking as this was so woebegone.

He paused on the opposite side of his desk from her, gave a soft salute, and smiled. 'What's your name, my dear?'

She drew a shaken breath. After trying several times, she managed to speak. 'I didn't think . . . anyone . . . understood my language.'

'A few of us do. The hypnopede, you know.' Evidently she did not know. He thought a short, dry lecture might soothe her. 'An invention made a few decades ago on our planet. Suppose another person and I have no language in common. We can be given a drug to accelerate our nervous systems, and then the machine flashes images on a screen and analyzes the sounds uttered by the other person. What it hears is transferred to me and impressed on the speech center of my brain, electronically. As the vocabulary grows, a computer in the machine figures out the structure of the whole language – semantics, grammar, and so on – and orders my own learning accordingly. That way, a few short, daily sessions make me fluent.'

She touched her lips with a tongue that seemed equally parched. 'I heard once . . . of some experiments at the University,' she whispered. 'They never got far. No reason for such a machine. Only one language on Vaynamo.'

'And on Chertkoi. But we've already subjugated two other planets, one of 'em divided into hundreds of language groups. And we expect there'll be others.' Golyev opened a drawer, took out a bottle and two glasses. 'Care for brandy?'

He poured. 'I'm Bors Golyev, an astronautical executive of the Interplanetary Corporation, commanding this scout force,' he said. 'Who are you?'

She didn't answer. He reached a glass toward her. 'Come, now,' he said, 'I'm not such a bad fellow. Here, drink. To our better acquaintance.'

With a convulsive movement, she struck the glass from his hand. It bounced on the floor. 'Almighty Creator! No!' she yelled. 'You murdered my husband!'

She stumbled to a chair, fell down in it, rested head in arms on the desk and began to weep. The spilled brandy crept across the floor toward her.

Golyev groaned. Why did he always get cases like this? Glebs Narov, now, had clapped hands on the jolliest tawny wench you could imagine, when they conquered Marsya on Imfan: delighted to be liberated from her own drab culture.

Well, he could kick this female back down among the other prisoners. But he didn't want to. He seated himself across from her, lit a cigar out of the box on his desk, and held his own glass to the light. Ruby smoldered within.

'I'm sorry,' he said. 'How was I to know? What's done is done. There wouldn't have been so many casualties if they'd been sensible and given up. We shot a few to prove we meant business, but then called on the rest over a loud-speaker, to yield. They didn't. For that matter, you were riding a six-legged animal out of the fields, I'm told. You came busting right *into* the fight. Why didn't you ride the other way and hide out till we left?'

'My husband was there,' she said after a silence. When she raised her face, he saw it gone cold and stiff. 'And our child.'

'Oh? Uh, maybe we picked up the kid, at least. If you'd like to go see – '

'No,' she said, toneless and yet somehow with a dim returning pride. 'I got Hauki away. I rode straight to the mansion and got him. Then one of your fire-guns hit the roof and the house began to burn. I told Huiva to take the baby – never mind where. I said I'd follow if I could. But Karlavi was out there, fighting. I went back to the barricade. He had been killed just a few seconds before. His face was all bloody. Then your cars broke through the barricade and someone caught me. But you don't have Hauki. Or Karlavi!'

As if drained by the effort of speech, she slumped and stared into a corner, empty-eyed.

'Well,' said Golyev, not quite comfortably, 'your people had been warned.' She didn't seem to hear him. 'You never got the message? But it was telecast over your whole planet. After our first non-secret landing. That was several days ago. Were you out in the woods or something? – Yes, we scouted telescopically, and made clandestine landings, and caught a few citizens to interrogate. But when we understood the situation, more or less, we landed openly in, uh, your city. Yuvaskula, is that the name? We seized it without too much damage, captured some officials of the planetary government, claimed the planet for IP and called on all citizens to cooperate. But they wouldn't! Why, one ambush alone cost us fifty good men. What could we do? We had to teach a lesson. We announced we'd punish a few random villages. That's more humane than bombarding from space with cobalt missiles. Isn't it? But I suppose your people didn't really believe us, the way they came swarming when we landed. Trying to parley with us first, and then trying to resist us with hunting rifles! What would you expect to happen?'

119

His voice seemed to fall into an echoless well.

He loosened his collar, which felt a trifle tight, took a deep drag on his cigar and refilled his glass. 'Of course, I don't expect you to see our side of it at once,' he said reasonably. 'You've been jogging along, isolated, for centuries, haven't you? Hardly a spaceship has touched at your planet since it was first colonized. You have none of your own, except a couple of interplanetary boats which hardly ever get used. That's what your President told me, and I believe him. Why should you go outsystem? You have everything you can use, right on your own world. The nearest sun to yours with an oxygen atmosphere planet is three parsecs off. Even with a very high-powered agoratron, you'd need ten years to get there, another decade to get back. A whole generation! Sure, the time-contraction effect would keep you young – ship's time for the voyage would only be a few weeks, or less – but all your friends would be middle-aged when you came home. Believe me, it's lonely being a spaceman.'

He drank. A pleasant burning went down his throat. 'No wonder men spread so slowly into space, and each colony is so isolated,' he said. 'Chertkoi is a mere name in your archives. And yet it's only fifteen light-years from Vaynamo. You can see our sun on any clear night. A reddish one. You call it Gamma Navarchi. Fifteen little light-years, and yet there's been no contact between our two planets for four centuries or more!

'So why now? Well, that's a long story. Let's just say Chertkoi isn't as friendly a world as Vaynamo. You'll see that for yourself. We, our ancestors, we came up the hard way, we had to struggle for everything. And now there are four billion of us! That was the census figure when I left. It'll probably be five billion when I get home. We have to have more resources. Our economy is grinding to a halt. And we can't afford economic dislocation. Not on as thin a margin as Chertkoi allows us. First we went back to the other planets of our system and worked them as much as practicable. Then we started re-exploring the nearer stars. So far we've found two useful planets. Yours is the third. You know what your population is? Ten million, your President claimed. Ten million people for a whole world of forests, plains, hills, oceans . . . why, your least continent has more natural resources than all Chertkoi. And you've stabilized at that population. You don't want more people!'

Golyev struck the desk with a thumb. 'If you think ten million stagnant agriculturists have a right to monopolize all that room and wealth, when four billion Chertkoians live on the verge of starvation,' he said indignantly, 'you can think again.'

She stirred. Not looking at him, her tone small and very distant, she said, 'It's our planet, to do with as we please. If you want to breed like maggots, you must take the consequences.'

Anger flushed the last sympathy from Golyev. He ground out his cigar in the ashwell and tossed off his brandy. 'Never mind moralizing,' he said. 'I'm no martyr. I became a spaceman because it's fun.'

He got up and walked around the desk to her.

## 538 A.C.C.:

When she couldn't stand the apartment any more, Elva went out on the balcony and looked across Dirzh until that view became unedurable in its turn.

From this height, the city had a certain grandeur. On every side it stretched horizonward, immense gray blocks among which rose an occasional spire shining with steel and glass. Eastward at the every edge of vision it ended before some mine pits, whose scaffolding and chimneys did not entirely cage off a glimpse of primordial painted desert. Between the buildings went a network of elevated trafficways, some carrying robofreight, others pullulating with gray-clad clients on foot. Overhead, against a purple-black sky and the planet's single huge moon, nearly full tonight, flitted the firefly aircars of executives, engineers, military techs, and others in the patron class. A few stars were visible, but the fever-flash of neon drowned most of them. Even by full red-tinged daylight, Elva could never see all the way downward. A fog of dust, smoke, fumes and vapors hid the bottom of the artificial mountains. She could only imagine the underground, caves and tunnels where workers of the lowest category were bred to spend their lives tending machines, and where a criminal class slunk about in armed packs.

It was rarely warm on Chertkoi, summer or winter. As the night wind gusted, Elva drew more tightly around her a mantle of genuine fur from Novagal. Bors wasn't stingy about clothes or jewels. But then, he liked to take her out in public places, where she could be admired and he envied. For the first few months she had refused to leave the apartment. He hadn't made an issue of it, only waited. In the end she gave in. Nowadays she looked forward eagerly to such times; they took her away from these walls. But of late there had been no celebrations. Bors was working too hard.

The moon Drogoi climbed higher, reddened by the hidden sun and the lower atmosphere of the city. At the zenith it would be pale copper. Once Elva had fancied the markings on it formed a death's head. They didn't really; that had just been her horror of everything Chertkoian. But she had never shaken off the impression.

She hunted among the constellations, knowing that if she found Vaynamo's sun it would hurt, but unable to stop. The air was too thick tonight, though, with an odor of acid and rotten eggs. She remembered riding out along Lake Rovaniemi, soon after her marriage. Karlavi was along: no one else, for you didn't need a bodyguard on Vaynamo. The two moons climbed fast. Their light made a trembling double bridge on the water. Trees rustled, the air smelled green, something sang with a liquid plangency, far off among moon-dappled shadows.

'But that's beautiful!' she whispered. 'Yonder songbird. We haven't anything like it in Ruuyalka.'

Karlavi chuckled. 'No bird at all. The Alfavala name – well, who can pronounce that? We humans say "yanno". A little pseudomammal, a terrible pest. Roots up tubers. For a while we thought we'd have to wipe out the species.'

'But they sing so sweetly.'

'True. Also, the Alfavala would be hurt. Insofar as they have anything like a religion, the yanno seems to be part of it, locally. Important to them somehow, at least.' Unspoken was the law under which she and he had both been raised: The green dwarfs are barely where man was two or three million years ago on Old Earth, but they are the real natives of Vaynamo, and if we share their planet, we're bound to respect them and help them.

Once Elva had tried to explain the idea to Bors Golyev. He couldn't understand at all. If the abos occupied land men might use, why not hunt them off it? They'd make good, crafty game, wouldn't they?

'Can anything be done about the yanno?' she asked Karlavi.

'For several generations, we fooled around with electric fences and so on. But just a few years ago, I consulted Paaska Ecological Institute and found they'd developed a wholly new approach to such problems. They can now tailor a dominant mutant gene which produces a strong distaste for Vitamin C. I suppose you know Vitamin C isn't part of native biochemistry, but occurs only in plants of Terrestrial origin. We released the mutants to breed, and every season there are fewer yanno that'll touch our crops. In another five years there'll be too few to matter.'

'And they'll still sing for us.' She edged her hailu closer to his. Their knees touched. He leaned over and kissed her.

Elva shivered. *I'd better go in,* she thought.

The light switched on automatically as she re-entered the living-room. At least artificial illumination on Chertkoi was like home. Dwelling under different suns had not yet changed human eyes. Though in other respects, man's colonies had drifted far apart indeed . . . The apartment had three cramped rooms, which was considered luxurious. When five billion people, more every day, grabbed their living from a planet as bleak as this, even the wealthy must do without things that were the natural right of the poorest Vaynamoan – spaciousness, trees, grass beneath bare feet, your own house and an open sky. Of course, Chertkoi had very sophisticated amusements to offer in exchange, everything from multisensory films to live combats.

Belgoya pattered in from her offside cubicle. Elva wondered if the maidservant ever slept. 'Does the mistress wish anything, please?'

'No.' Elva sat down. She ought to be used to the gravity by now, she thought. How long had she been here? A years, more or less. She hadn't kept track of time, especially when they used an unfamiliar calendar. Denser than Vaynamo, Chertkoi exerted a ten percent greater surface pull; but that wasn't enough to matter, when you were in good physical condition. Yet she was always tired.

'No, I don't want anything.' She leaned back on the couch and rubbed her eyes. The haze outside had made them sting.

'A cup of stim, perhaps, if the mistress please?' The girl bowed some more, absurdly doll-like in her uniform.

'No!' Elva shouted. 'Go away!'

'I beg your pardon. I am a worm. I implore your magnanimity'. Terrified, the maid crawled backward out of the room on her belly.

Elva lit a cigaret. She hadn't smoked on Vaynamo, but since coming here she'd take it up, become a chain-smoker like most Chertkoians who could afford it. You needed something to do with your hands. The servility of clients toward patrons no longer shocked her, but rather made her think of them as faintly slimy. To be sure, one could see the reasons. Belgoya, for instance, could be fired any time and sent back to the street level.

Down there were a million eager applicants for her position. Elva forgot her and reached after the teleshow dials. Something must be on, loud and full of action, something to watch, something to do with her evening.

The door opened. Elva turned about, tense with expectation. So Bors was home. And alone. If he'd brought a friend along, she would have had to go into the sleeping cubicle and merely listen. Upper-class Chertkoians didn't like women intruding on their conversation. But Bors alone meant she would have someone to talk to.

He came in, his tread showing he was also tired. He skimmed his hat into a corner and dropped his cloak on the floor. Belgoya crept forth to pick them up. As he sat down, she was there with a drink and a cigar.

Elva waited. She knew his moods. When the blunt, bearded face had lost some of its hardness, she donned a smile and stretched herself along the couch, leaning on one elbow. 'You've been working yourself to death,' she scolded.

He sighed. 'Yeh. But the end's in view. Another week, and all the damn paperwork will be cleared up.'

'You hope. One of your bureaucrats will probably invent nineteen more forms to fill out in quadruplicate.'

'Probably.'

'We never had that trouble at home. The planetary government was only a coordinating body with strictly limited powers. Why won't you people even consider establishing something similar?'

'You know the reasons. Five billion of them. You've got room to be an individual on Vaynamo.' Golyev finished his drink and held the glass out for a refill. 'By all chaos! I'm tempted to desert when we get there.'

Elva lifted her brows. 'That's a thought,' she purred.

'Oh, you know it's impossible,' he said, returning to his usual humorlessness. 'Quite apart from the fact I'd be one enemy alien on an entire planet –'

'Not necessarily.'

' – All right, even if I got naturalized (and who wants to become a clodhopper?) I'd have only thirty years till the Third Expedition came. I don't want to be a client in my old age. Or worse, see my children made clients.'

Elva lit a second cigaret from the stub of the first. She drew in the smoke hard enough to hollow her cheeks.

*But it's fine to launch the Second Expedition and make clients*

124

*of others,* she thought. *The first, that captured me and a thousand more (What's become of them? How many are dead, how many found useless and sent lobotomized to the mines, how many are still being pumped dry of information?) . . . that was a mere scouting trip. The Second will have fifty warships, and try to force surrender. At the very least, it will flatten all possible defenses, destroy all imaginable war potential, bring back a whole herd of slaves. And then the Third, a thousand ships or more, will bring the final conquest, the garrisons, the overseers and entrepreneurs and colonists. But that won't be for forty-five years or better from tonight. A man on Vaynamo . . . Hauki . . . a man who survives the coming of the Second Expedition will have thirty-odd years left in which to be free. But will he dare have children?*

'I'll settle down there after the Third Expedition, I think,' Golyev admitted. 'From what I saw of the planet last time, I believe I'd like it. And the opportunities are unlimited. A whole world waiting to be properly developed!'

'I could show you a great many chances you'd otherwise overlook,' insinuated Elva.

Golyev shifted position. 'Let's not go into that again,' he said. 'You know I can't take you along.'

'You're the fleet commander, aren't you?'

'Yes, I will be, but curse it, can't you understand? The IP is not like any other corporation. We use men who think and act on their own, not planet-hugging morons like what's-her-name – ' he jerked a thumb at Belgoya, who lowered her eyes meekly and continued mixing him a third drink. 'Men of patron status, younger sons of executives and engineers. The officers can't have special privileges. It'd ruin morale.'

Elva fluttered her lashes. 'Not that much. Really.'

'My oldest boy's promised to take care of you. He's not such a bad fellow as you seem to think. You only have to go along with his whims. I'll see you again, in thirty years.'

'When I'm gray and wrinkled. Why not kick me out in the street and be done?'

'You know why,' he said ferociously. 'You're the first woman I could ever talk to. No, I'm not bored with you! But – '

'If you really cared for me – '

'What kind of idiot do you take me for? I know you're planning to sneak away to your own people, once we've landed.'

Elva tossed her head, haughtily. 'Well! If you believe that of me, there's nothing more to say.'

125

'Aw, now, sweetling, don't take that attitude.' He reached out a hand to lay on her arm. She withdrew to the far end of the couch. He looked baffled.

'Another thing,' he argued. 'If you care about your planet at all, as I suppose you do, even if you've now seen what a bunch of petrified mudsuckers they are — remember, what we'll have to do there won't be pretty.'

'First you call me a traitor,' she flared, 'and now you say I'm gutless!'

'Hoy, wait a minute —'

'Go on, beat me. I can't stop you. You're brave enough for that.'

'I never —'

In the end, he yielded.


## 553 A.C.C.:

The missile which landed on Yuvaskula had a ten-kilometer radius of total destruction. Thus most of the city went up in one radioactive fire-gout. In a way, the thought of men and women and little children with pet kittens, incinerated, made a trifle less pain in Elva than knowing the Old Town was gone: the cabin raised by the first men to land on Vaynamo, the ancient church of St Yarvi with its stained-glass windows and gilded belltower, the Museum of Art where she went as a girl on entranced visits, the University where she studied and where she met Karlavi — *I'm a true daughter of Vaynamo,* she thought with remorse. *Whatever is traditional, full of memories, whatever has been looked at and been done by all the generations before me, I hold dear. The Chertkoians don't care. They haven't any past worth remembering.*

Flames painted the northern sky red, even at this distance, as she walked among the pastishelters of the advanced base. She had flown within a hundred kilometers, using an aircar borrowed from the flagship, then landed to avoid possible missiles and hitched a ride here on a supply truck. The Chertkoian enlisted men aboard had been delighted until she showed them her pass, signed by Commander Golyev himself. Then they became cringingly respectful.

The pass was only supposed to let her move freely about in the rear areas, and she'd had enough trouble wheedling it from

Bors. But no one thereafter looked closely at it. She herself was so unused to the concept of war that she didn't stop to wonder at such lax security measures. Had she done so, she would have realized Chertkoi had never developed anything better, never having faced an enemy of comparable strength. Vaynamo certainly wasn't, even though the planet was proving a hard-shelled opponent, with every farmhouse a potential arsenal and every forest road a possible death trap. Guerrilla fighters hindered the movements of an invader with armor, atomic artillery, complete control of air and space; they could not stop him.

Eva drew her dark mantle more tightly about her and crouched under a gun emplacement. A sentry went by, his helmet square against the beloved familiar face of a moon, his rifle aslant across the stars. She didn't want needless questioning. For a moment the distant blaze sprang higher, unrestful ruddy light touched her, she was afraid she had been observed. But the man continued his round.

From the air she had seen that the fire was mostly a burning forest, kindled from Yuvaskula. Those wooden houses not blown apart by the missile stood unharmed in the whitest glow. Some process must have been developed at one of the research institutes, for indurating timber, since she left . . . How Bors would laugh if she told him. An industry which turned out a bare minimum of vehicles, farm machinery, tools, chemicals; a science which developed fireproofing techniques and traced out ecological chains; a population which deliberately held itself static, so as to preserve its old customs and laws – presuming to make war on Chertkoi!

Even so, he was too experienced a fighter to dismiss any foe as weak without careful examination. He had been excited enough about one thing to mention it to Elva – a prisoner taken in a skirmish near Yuvaskula, when he still hoped to capture the city intact: an officer, who cracked just enough under interrogation to indicate he knew something important. But Golyev couldn't wait around for the inquisitors to finish their work. He must go out the very next day to oversee the battle for Lempo Machine Tool Works, and Elva knew he wouldn't return soon. The plant had been constructed underground as an economy measure, and to preserve the green parkscape above. Now its concrete warrens proved highly defensible, and were being bitterly contested. The Chertkoians meant to seize it, so they could be sure of demolishing everything. They would not leave Vaynamo any nucleus of industry. After all, the planet would have thirty-odd years to recover and rearm itself against the Third Expedition.

Left alone by Bors, Elva took an aircar and slipped off to the advanced base.

She recognized the plastishelter she wanted by its Intelligence insignia. The guard outside aimed a rifle at her. 'Halt!' His boyish voice cracked over with nervousness. More than one sentry had been found in the morning with his throat cut.

'It's all right,' she told him. 'I'm to see the prisoner Ivalo.'

'The gooze officer?' He flashed a pencil-thin beam across her face. 'But you're a – uh –'

'A Vaynamoan myself. Of course. There are a few of us along, you know. Prisoners taken last time, who've enlisted in your cause as guides and spies. You must have heard of me. I'm Elva, Commander Golyev's lady.'

'Oh. Yes, mistress. Sure I have.'

'Here's my pass.'

He squinted at it uneasily. 'But, uh, may I ask what, uh, what *you* figure to do? I've got strict orders –'

Elva gave him her most confidential smile. 'My own patron had the idea. The prisoner is withholding valuable information. He has been treated roughly, but resisted. Now, all at once, we'll take the pressure off. An attractive woman of his own race . . . '

'I get it. Maybe he will crack. I dunno, though, mistress. These slant-eyed towheads are mean animals – begging your pardon! Go right on in. Holler if he gets rough or, or anything.'

The door was unlocked for her. Elva went on through, into a hemicylindrical room so low that she must stoop. A lighting tube switched on, showing a pallet laid across the floor.

Captain Ivalo was gray at the temples, but still tough and supple. His face had gone haggard, sunken eyes and a stubble of beard; his garments were torn and filthy. When he looked up, coming awake, he was too exhausted to show much surprise. 'What now?' he said in dull Chertkoian. 'What are you going to try next?'

Elva answered in Vaynamoan (oh, God, it was a year and a half, her own time, nearly seventeen years cosmic time, since she had uttered a word to anyone from her planet): 'Be quiet. I beg you. We mustn't be suspected.'

He sat up. 'Who are you?' he snapped. His own Vaynamoan accent was faintly pedantic; he must be a teacher or scientist in that peacetime life which now seemed so distant. 'A collaborator? I understand there are some. Every barrel must hold a few rotten apples, I suppose.'

She sat down on the floor near him, hugged her knees and stared at the curving wall. 'I don't know what to call myself,' she said tonelessly. 'I'm with them, yes. But they captured me the last time.'

He whistled, a soft note. One hand reached out, not altogether steady, and stopped short of touching her. 'I was young then,' he said. 'But I remember. Do I know your family?'

'Maybe. I'm Elva, daughter of Byarmo, the Magnate of Ruuyalka. My husband was Karlavi, the Freeholder of Tervola.' Suddenly she couldn't stay controlled. She grasped his arm so hard that her nails drew blood. 'Do you know what became of my son? His name was Hauki. I got him away, in care of an Alfa servant. Hauki, Karlavi's son, Freeholder of Tervola. Do you know?'

He disengaged himself as gently as possible and shook his head. 'I'm sorry. I've heard of both places, but only as names. I'm from the Aakinen Islands myself.'

Her head drooped.

'Ivalo is my name,' he said clumsily.

'I know.'

'What?'

'Listen.' She raised her eyes to him. They were quite dry. 'I've been told you have important information.'

He bridled. 'If you think –'

'No. Please listen. Here.' She fumbled in a pocket of her gown. At last her fingers closed on the vial. She held it out to him. 'An antiseptic. But the label says it's very poisonous if taken internally. I brought it for you.'

He stared at her for a long while.

'It's all I can do,' she mumbled, looking away again.

He took the bottle and turned it over and over in his hands. The night grew silent around them.

Finally he asked, 'Won't you suffer for this?'

'Not too much.'

'Wait . . . If you could get in here, you can surely escape completely. Our troops can't be far off. Or any farmer hereabouts will hide you.'

She shook her head. 'No. I'll stay with them. Maybe I can help in some other small way. What else has there been to keep me alive, but the hope of – It wouldn't be any better, living here, if we're all conquered. There's to be a final attack, three decades hence. Do you know that?'

'Yes. Our side takes prisoners too, and quizzes them. The first episode puzzled us. Many thought it had only been a raid by — what's the word? — by pirates. But now we know they really do intend to take our planet away.'

'You must have developed some good linguists,' she said, seeking impersonality. 'To be able to talk with your prisoners. Of course, you yourself, after capture, could be educated by the hypnopede.'

'The what?'

'The language-teaching machine.'

'Oh, yes, the enemy do have them, don't they? But we do too. After the first raid, those who thought there was a danger the aliens might come back set about developing such machines. I knew Chertkoian weeks before my own capture.'

'I wish I could help you escape,' she said dully. 'But I don't know how. That bottle is all I can do. Isn't it?'

'Yes.' He regarded the thing with a fascination.

'My patron — Golyev himself — said his men would rip you open to get your knowledge. So I thought — '

'You're very kind,' Ivalo grimaced, as if he had tasted something foul. 'But your act may turn out pointless. I don't know anything useful. I wasn't even sworn to secrecy about what I do know. Why've I held out, then? Don't ask me. Stubbornness. Anger. Or just hating to admit that my people — our people, damn it! — that they could be so weak and foolish.'

'What?' Her glance jerked up to him.

'They could win the war at a stroke,' he said. 'They won't. They'd rather die, and let their children be enslaved by the Third Expedition.'

'What do you mean?' She crouched to hands and knees, bowstring-tense.

He shrugged. 'I told you, a number of people on Vaynamo took the previous invasion at its word, that it was the vanguard of a conquering army. There was no official action. How could there be, with a government as feeble as ours? But some of the research biologists — '

'Not a plague!'

'Yes. Mutated from the local coryzoid virus. Incubation period, approximately one month, during which time it's contagious. Vaccination is still effective two weeks after exposure, so all our people could be safeguarded. But the Chertkoians would

130

take the disease back with them. Estimated deaths, ninety percent of the race.'

'But – '

'That's where the government did step in,' he said with bitterness. 'The information was suppressed. The virus cultures were
destroyed. The theory was, even to save ourselves we couldn't do
such a thing.'

Elva felt the tautness leave her. She sagged. She had seen
small children on Chertkoi too.

'They're right, of course,' she said wearily.

'Perhaps. Perhaps. And yet we'll be overrun and butchered,
or reduced to serfdom. Won't we? Our forests will be cut down,
our mines gutted, our poor Alfavala exterminated . . . To hell
with it.' Ivalo gazed at the poison vial. 'I don't have any scientific data, I'm not a virologist. It can't do any military harm to
tell the Chertkoians. But I've seen what they've done to us. I
would give them the sickness.'

'I wouldn't.' Elva bit her lip.

He regarded her for a long time. 'Won't you escape? Never
mind being a planetary heroine. There's nothing you can do.
The invaders will go home when they've wrecked all our industry. They won't come again for thirty years. You can be free
most of your life.'

'You forget,' she said, 'that if I leave with them, and come
back, the time for me will only have been one or two years.' She
sighed. 'I can't help make ready for the next battle. I'm just a
woman. Untrained. While maybe . . . oh, if nothing else, there'll
be more Vaynamoan prisoners brought to Chertkoi. I have a tiny
bit of influence. Maybe I can help them.'

Ivalo considered the poison. 'I was about to use this anyway,'
he muttered. 'I didn't think staying alive was worth the trouble.
But now – if you can – No.' He gave the vial back to her. 'I
thank you, my lady.'

'I have an idea,' she said, with a hint of color in her voice.
'Go ahead and tell them what you know. Pretend I talked you
into it. Then I might be able to get you exchanged. It's barely
possible.'

'Oh, perhaps,' he said, not believing. 'I'll try.'

She rose to go. 'If you are set free,' she stammered, 'will you
make a visit to Tervola? Will you find Hauki, Karlavi's son,
and tell him you saw me? If he's alive.'

Dirzh had changed while the ships were away. The evolution
continued after their return. The city grew bigger, smokier,
uglier. More people each year dropped from client status, went
underground and joined the gangs. Occasionally, these days, the
noise and vibration of pitched battles down in the tunnels could
be detected up on patron level. The desert could no longer be
seen, even from the highest towers, only the abandoned mine
and the slag mountains, in process of conversation to tenements.
The carcinogenic murkiness crept upward until it could be
smelled on the most elite balconies. Teleshows got noisier and
nakeder, to compete with live performances, which were now
offering more elaborate bloodlettings than old-fashioned combats. The news from space was of a revolt suppressed on
Novagal, resulting in such an acute labor shortage that workers
were drafted from Imfan and shipped thither.

Only when you looked at the zenith was there no apparent
change. The daylit sky was still cold purplish-blue, with an
occasional yellow dustcloud. At night there were still the stars,
and a skull.

And yet, thought Elva, you wouldn't need a large telescope
to see the Third Expedition fleet in orbit – eleven hundred spacecraft, the unarmed ones loaded with troops and equipment,
nearly the whole strength of Chertkoi marshaling to conquer
Vaynamo. Campaigning across interstellar distances wasn't easy.
You couldn't send home for supplies or reinforcements. You
broke the enemy or he broke you. Fleet Admiral Bors Golyev
did not intend to be broken.

He did not even plan to go home with news of a successful
probing operation or a successful raid. The Third Expedition
was to be final. And he must allow for the Vaynamoans having
had a generation in which to recuperate. He'd smashed their
heavy industry, but if they were really determined, they could
have rebuilt. No doubt a space fleet of some kind would be
waiting to oppose him.

He knew it couldn't be of comparable power. Ten million
people, forced to recreate all their mines and furnaces and
factories before they could lay the keel of a single boat, had no
possibility of matching the concerted efforts of six and a half
billion whose world had been continuously industrialized for
centuries, and who could draw on the resources of two subject
planets. Sheer mathematics ruled it out. But the ten million

could accomplish something; and nuclear-fusion missiles were some degree an equalizer. Therefore Bors Golyev asked for so much strength that the greatest conceivable enemy force would be swamped. And he got it.

Elva leaned on the balcony rail. A chill wind fluttered her gown around her, so that the rainbow hues rippled and ran into each other. She had to admit the fabric was lovely. Bors tried hard to please her. (Though why must he mention the price?) He was so childishly happy himself, at his accomplishments, at his new eminence, at the eight-room apartment which he now rated on the very heights of the Lebedan Tower.

'Not that we'll be here long,' he had said, after they first explored its intricacies. 'My son Nivko has done good work in the home office. That's how come I got this command; experience alone wasn't enough. Of course, he'll expect me to help along his sons . . . But anyhow, the Third Expedition can go even sooner than I'd hoped. Just a few months, and we're on our way.'

'We?' murmured Elva.

'You do want to come, don't you?'

'The last voyage, you weren't so eager.'

'Uh, yes. I did have a deuce of a time, too, getting you aboard. But this'll be different. First, I've got so much rank I'm beyond criticism, even beyond jealousy. And second, well, you count too. You're not any picked-up native female. You're Elva! The girl who on her own hook got that fellow Ivalo to confess.'

She turned her head slightly, regarding him sideways from droop-lidded blue eyes. Under the ruddy sun, her hair turned to raw gold. 'I should think the news would have alarmed them, here on Chertkoi,' she said. 'Being told that they nearly brought their own extinction about. I wonder that they dare launch another attack.'

Golyev grinned. 'You should have heard the ruckus. Some Directors did vote to keep hands off Vaynamo. Others wanted to sterilize the whole planet with cobalt missiles. But I talked 'em around. Once we've beaten the fleet and occupied the planet, its whole population will be hostage for good behavior. We'll make examples of the first few goozes who give us trouble of any sort. Then they'll know we mean what we say when we announce our policy. At the first suspicion of plague among us, we'll lay waste a continent. If the suspicion is confirmed, we'll bombard the whole works. No, there won't be any bug warfare.'

'I know. I've heard your line of reasoning before. About five hundred times, in fact.'

'Destruction! Am I really that much of a bore?' He came up behind her and laid his hands on her shoulders. 'I don't mean to be. Honest. I'm not used to talking to women that's all.'

'And I'm not used to being shut away like a prize fish, except when you want to exhibit me,' she said sharply.

He kissed her neck. His whiskers tickled. 'It'll be different on Vaynamo. When we're settled down. I'll be governor of the planet. The Directorate has as good as promised me. Then I can do as I want. And so can you.'

'I doubt that. Why should I believe anything you say? When I told you I'd made Ivalo talk by promising you would exchange him, you wouldn't keep the promise.' She tried to wriggle free, but his grip was too strong. She contented herself with going rigid. 'Now, when I tell you the prisoners we brought back this time are to be treated like human beings, you whine about your damned Directorate – '

'But the Directorate makes policy!'

'You're the Fleet Admiral, as you never lose a chance to remind me. You can certainly bring pressure to bear. You can insist the Vaynamoans be taken out of those kennels and given honorable detention – '

'Awww, now.' His lips nibbled along her cheek. She turned her head away and continued:

' – and you can get what you insist on. They're your own prisoners, aren't they? I've listened enough to you, and your dreary officers when you brought them home. I've read books, hundreds of books. What else have I got to do, day after day and week after week?'

'But I'm busy! I'd like to take you out, honest, but – '

'So I understand the power structure on Chertkoi just as well as you do, Bors Golyev. If not better. If you don't know how to use your influence, then slough off some of that conceit, sit down and listen while I tell you how.'

'Well, uh, I never denied, sweetling, you've given me some advice from time to time.'

'So listen to me. I say all the Vaynamoans you hold are to be given decent quarters, recreation, and respect. What did you capture them for, if not to get some use out of them? And the proper use is not to titillate yourself by kicking them around. A dog would serve that purpose better.

'Furthermore, the fleet has to carry them back to Vaynamo. All of them.'

'What? You don't know what you're talking about! The logistics is tough enough without – '

'I do so know what I'm talking about. Which is more than I can say for you. You want guides, intermediaries, puppet leaders, don't you? Not by the score, a few cowards and traitors, as you have hitherto. You need hundreds. Well, there they are, right in your hands.'

'And hating my guts.'

'Give them reasonable living conditions and they won't. Not quite so much, anyhow. Then bring them back home – a generation after they left, all their friends aged or dead, everything altered once you've conquered the planet. And let me deal with them. You'll get helpers.'

'Uh, well, uh, I'll think about it.'

'You'll do something about it!' She eased her body leaning back against the rubbery muscles of his chest. Her face turned upward, with a slow smile. 'You're good at doing things, Bors.'

'Oh, Elva – '

Later: 'You know one thing I want to do? As soon as I'm well established in the governorship? I want to marry you. Properly and openly. Let 'em be shocked. I won't care. I want to be your husband, and the father of your kids, Elva. How's that sound? Mistress Governor General Elva Golyev of Vaynamo Planetary Province. Never thought you'd get that far in life, did you?'

*583 A.C.C.:*

As they neared the end of the journey, he sent her to his cabin. An escape suit – an armored cylinder with propulsors, air regenerator, food and water supplies, which she could enter in sixty seconds – occupied most of the room. 'Not that I expect any trouble,' he said. 'But if something should happen . . . I hope you can make it down to the surface.' He paused. The officers on the bridge moved quietly about their tasks; the engines droned; the distorted stars of near-light velocity framed his hard brown face. There was a thin sheen of sweat on his skin; not fear, but an effort to say something.

'I love you, you know,' he finished. Quickly, he turned back to his duties. Elva went below.

135

Clad in a spaceman's uniform, seated on the bank, enclosed in toning metal, she felt the inward wrench as the agoratron went off and speed was converted back to atomic mass. The cabin's private viewscreen showed stars in their proper constellations again, needle-sharp against blackness. Vaynamo was tiny and blue, still several hundred thousand kilometers remote. Elva ran fingers through her hair. The scalp beneath felt tight, and her lips were dry. A person couldn't help being afraid, she thought. Just a little afraid.

She called up the memory of Karlavi's land, where he had now lain for sixty-two years. Reeds whispered along the shores of Rovaniemi, the wind made a rippling in long grass, and it was time again for the lampflowers to blow, all down the valley. Dreamlike at the edge of vision, the snowpeaks of the High Mikkela floated in an utter blue.

*I'm coming back, Karlavi,* she thought.

In her screen, the nearer vessels were glinting toys, plunging through emptiness. The further ones were not visible at this low magnification. Only the senses of radar, gravpulse, and less familiar creations, analyzed by whirling electrons in a computer bank, gave any approach to reality. But she could listen in on the main intercom line to the bridge if she chose, and hear those data spoken. She flipped the switch. Nothing yet, only routine reports. Had the planet's disc grown a trifle?

*Have I been wrong all the time?* she thought. Her heart stopped for a second.

Then: 'Alert! Condition red! Alert! Condition red! Objects detected, approaching nine-thirty o'clock, fifteen degrees high. Neutrino emissions indicate nuclear engines.'

'Alert! Condition yellow! Quiescent object detected in orbit about target planet, two-thirty o'clock, ten degrees low, circa 75,000 kilometers distant. Extremely massive. Repeat, quiescent. Low level of nuclear activity, but at bolometric temperature of ambient space. Possibly an abandoned space fortress, except for being so massive.'

'Detected objects identified as space craft. Approaching with average radial velocity of 250 KPS. No evident deceleration. Number very large, estimated at five thousand. All units small, about the mass of our scoutboats.'

The gabble went on until Golyev's voice cut through: 'Attention! Fleet Admiral to bridge of all units. Now hear this.' Sardonically: 'The opposition is making a good try. Instead of building any real ships – they could only have constructed a few at best – they've turned out thousands of manned warboats. Their plan is obviously to cut through our formation, relying on speed, and release tracking torps in quantity. Stand by to repel. We have enough detectors, antimissiles, negafields, to overwhelm them in this department too. Once past us, the boats will need hours to decelerate and come back within decent shooting range. By that time we should be in orbit around the planet. Be alert for possible emergencies, of course. But I only expect standard operations will be necessary. Good shooting!'

Elva strained close to her screen. All at once she saw the Vaynamoan fleet, sparks, but a horde of them, twinkling among the stars. Closer! Her fingers strained against each other. *They must have some plan,* she told herself. *If I'm blown up in five minutes – I was hoping I'd get down to you, Karlavi. But if I don't, good-bye, good-bye.*

The fleets neared each other: on the one side, ponderous dreadnaughts, cruisers, auxiliary warcraft, escorting swarms of transport and engineer ships; on the opposite side, needle-thin boats whose sole armour was velocity. The guns of Chertkoi swung about, hoping for a lucky hit. At such speeds it was improbable. The fleets would interpenetrate and pass in a fractional second. The Vaynamoans could not be blasted until they came to grips near their home world. However, if a nuclear shell should find its mark now – what blaze in heaven!

The flagship staggered.

'Engine room to bridge. What's happened?'

'Bridge to engine room. Gimme some power there! What in all destruction – ?'

'*Sharyats* to *Askol. Sharyats* to *Askol.* Am thrown off course, Accelerating. What's going on?'

'Look out!'

'*Fodorev* to *Zuevots*! Look alive, you bloody fool! You'll ram us!'

Cushioned by the internal field, Elva felt only the minutest fraction of that immense velocity change. Even so a wave of sickness went through her. She clutched at the bunk stanchion. The desk ripped from a loose mooring and crashed into the wall, which buckled. The deck split open underfoot. A roar went through the entire hull, ribs groaned as they bent, plates screamed as they sheared. A girder snapped in twain and spat sharp fragments among a gun turret crew. A section broke apart, air gushed out, a hundred men died before the sealing bulkheads could close.

After a moment, the stabilizing energies regained interior control. The images on Elva's screen steadied. She drew a shaken lungful of air and watched. Out of formation, the *Askol* plunged within a kilometer of her sister ship the *Zuevots* — just when that cyclopean hull smashed into the cruiser *Fodorev*. Fire sheeted as accumulator banks were shorted. The two giants crumpled, glowed white at the point of impact, fused, and spun off in a lunatic waltz. Men and supplies pinwheeled from the cracks gaping in them. Two gun turrets wrapped their long barrels around each other like intertwining snakes. Then the whole mess struck a third vessel. Steel chunks exploded into space.

Through the noise and the human screaming, Golyev's voice blasted. 'Pipe down there! Belay that! By Creation, I'll shoot the next man who whimpers! The enemy will be here in a minute. All stations, by the numbers, report.'

A measure of discipline returned. These were fighting men. Instruments fingered outward, the remaining computers whirred, minds made deductive leaps, gunners returned to their posts. The Vaynamoan fleet passed through, and the universe exploded in brief pyrotechnics. Many a Chertkoian ship died then, its defenses too battered, its defenders too stunned to ward off the tracking torpedoes. But others fought back, saved themselves, and saw their enemies vanish in the distance.

Still they tumbled off course, their engines helpless to free them. Elva heard a physicist's clipped tones give the deduction from his readings. The entire fleet had been caught in a cone of gravitational force emanating from that massive object detected in orbit. Like a maelstrom of astronomical dimensions, it had snatched them from their paths. Those closest and in the most intense field strength — a forth of the armada — had been wrecked by sheer deceleration. Now the force was drawing them down the vortex of itself.

'But that's impossible!' wailed the *Askol*'s chief engineer. 'A gravity attractor beam of that magnitude . . . Admiral, it can't be done! The power requirements would burn out any generator in a microsecond!'

'It's being done,' said Golyev harshly. 'Maybe they figured out a new way to feed energy into a space distorter. Now, where are those figures on intensity? And my slide rule . . . Yeh. The whole fleet will soon be in a field so powerful that — Well, we won't let it happen. Stand by to hit that generator with every- thing we've got.'

'But sir . . . we must have — I don't know how many ships — close enough to it now to be within total destruction radius.'

'Tough on them. Stand by. Gunnery Control, fire when ready.'

And then, whispered, even though that particular line was private and none else in the ship would hear: 'Elva. Are you all right down there? Elva!'

Her hands had eased their trembling enough for her to light a cigaret. She didn't speak. Let him worry. It might reduce his efficiency.

Her screen did not happen to face the vortex source, and thus did not show its destruction by the nuclear barrage. Not that that could have registered. The instant explosion of sun-center ferocity transcended any sense, human or electronic. Down on Vaynamo surface, in broad daylight, they must have turned dazzled eyes from that brilliance. Anyone within a thousand kilometers of those warheads died, no matter how much steel and force field he had interposed. Twoscore Chertkoian ships were suddenly manned by corpses. Those further in were fused to lumps. Still further in, they ceased to exist, save as gas at millions of degrees temperature. The vessels already crashed on the giant station were turned into unstable isotopes, their very atoms dying.

But the station itself vanished. And Vaynamo had only the capacity to build one such monster. The Chertkoian ships were free again.

'Admiral to all captains!' cried Golyev. 'Admiral to all captains. Let the reports wait. Clear the lines. I want every man in the fleet to hear me. Stand by for message.

'Now hear this. This is Supreme Commander Bors Golyev. We just took a rough blow, boys. The enemy had an unsuspected weapon, and cost us a lot of casualties. But we've destroyed the thing. I repeat, we blew it out of the cosmos. And I say, well done! I say also, we still have a hundred times the strength of the enemy, and he's shot his bolt. We're going on in. We're going to — '

'Alert! Condition red! Enemy boats returning. Enemy boats returning. Radial velocity circa 50 KPS, but acceleration circa 100 G.'

'What?'

Elva herself saw the Vaynamoan shooting stars come back into sight.

Golyev tried hard to shout down the panic of his officers.

Would they stop running around like old women? The enemy had developed something else, some method of accelerating at unheard-of rates under gravitational thrust. But not by witch-craft! It would be an internal-stress compensator developed to ultimate efficiency, plus an adaptation of whatever principle was used in the attractor vortex. Or it could be a breakthrough, a totally new principle, maybe something intermediate between the agoratron and the ordinary interplanetary drive . . . 'Never mind what, you morons! They're still only a flock of splinters! Kill them!'

But the armada was rolling about in blind confusion. The detectors had given more seconds of warning, which were lost in understanding that the warning was correct and in frantically seeking to rally men already shaken. Then the splinter fleet was in among the Chertkoians. It braked its furious relative velocity with a near-instantaneous quickness for which the Chertkoian gunners and gun computers had never been prepared. However, the Vaynamoan gunners were ready. And even a boat can carry torpedoes which will annihilate a battleship.

In a thousand fiery bursts, the armada died.

Not all of it. Unarmed craft were spared, if they would sur-render. Vaynamoan boarding parties freed such of their country-men as they found. The *Askol*, under Golyev's personal com-mand, stood off its attackers and moved doggedly outward, toward regions where it could use the agoratron to escape. The captain of a prize revealed that over a hundred Vaynamoans were aboard the flagship. So the attempt to blow it up was abandoned. Instead, a large number of boats shot dummy missiles, which kept the defense fully occupied. Meanwhile a companion force lay alongside, cut its way through the armor, and sent men in.

The Chertkoian crew resisted. But they were grossly out-numbered and outgunned. Most died, under bullets and grenades, gas and flame-throwers. Certain holdouts, who forti-fied a compartment, were welded in from the outside and left to starve or capitulate, whichever they chose. Even so, the *Askol* was so big that the boarding party took several hours to gain full possession.

The door opened. Elva stood up.

At first the half-dozen men who entered seemed foreign. In a minute – she was too tired and dazed to think clearly – she understood why. They were all in blue jackets and trousers, a uniform. She had never before seen two Vaynamoans dressed exactly alike. *But of course they would be,* she thought in a vague fashion. *We had to build a navy, didn't we?*

And they remained her own people: fair skin, straight hair, high cheekbones, tilted light eyes which gleamed all the brighter through the soot of battle. And, yes, they still walked like Vaynamoans, the swinging freeman's gait and the head held high, such as she had not seen for . . . for how long? So their clothes didn't matter, nor even the guns in their hands.

Slowly, through the ringing in her ears, she realized that the combat noise had stopped.

A young man in the lead took a step in her direction. 'My lady – ' he began.

'Is that her for certain?' asked someone else, less gently. 'Not a collaborator?'

A new man pushed his way through the squad. He was grizzled, pale from lack of sun, wearing a sleazy prisoner's coverall. But a smile touched his lips, and his bow to Elva was deep.

'This is indeed my lady of Tervola,' he said. To her: 'When these men released me, up in Section Fourteen, I told them we'd probably find you here. I am so glad.'

She needed a while to recognize him. 'Oh. Yes.' Her head felt heavy. It was all she could do to nod. 'Captain Ivalo. I hope you're all right.'

'I am, thanks to you, my lady. Someday we'll know how many hundreds of us are alive and sane – and here! – because of you.'

The squad leader made another step forward, sheathed his machine pistol and lifted both hands toward her. He was a well-knit, good-looking man, blond of hair, a little older than she: in his mid-thirties, perhaps. He tried to speak, but no words came out, and then Ivalo drew him back.

'In a moment,' said the ex-captive. 'Let's first take care of the unpleasant business.'

The leader hesitated, then, with a grimace, agreed. Two men shoved forward Bors Golyev. The admiral dripped blood from a dozen wounds and stumbled in his weariness. But when he saw Elva, he seemed to regain himself. 'You weren't hurt,' he breathed, as if the words were holy. 'I was so afraid . . . '

Ivalo said like steel: 'I've explained the facts of this case to the squad officer here, as well as his immediate superior. I'm sure you'll join us in our wish not to be inhumane, my lady. And yet a criminal trial in the regular courts would publicize matters

141

best forgotten and could only give him a limited punishment. So we, here and now, under the conditions of war and in view of your high services – '

The squad officer interrupted. He was white about the nostrils. 'Anything you order, my lady,' he said. 'You pass the sentence. We'll execute it at once.'

'Elva,' whispered Golyev.

She stared at him, remembering fire and enslavements and a certain man dead on a barricade. But everything seemed distant, not quite real.

'There's been too much suffering already,' she said.

She pondered a few seconds. 'Just take him out and shoot him.'

The officer looked relieved. He led his men forth. Golyev started to speak, but was hustled away too fast.

Ivalo remained in the cabin. 'My lady – ' He began, slow and awkward.

'Yes?' As her weariness overwhelmed her, Elva sat down again on the bunk. She fumbled for a cigaret. There was no emotion in her, only a dull wish for sleep.

'I've wondered . . . Don't answer this if you don't want to. You've been through so much.'

'That's all right,' she said mechanically. 'The trouble is over now, isn't it? I mean, we mustn't let the past obsess us.'

'Of course. Uh, they tell me Vaynamo hasn't changed much. The defense effort was bound to affect society somewhat, but they've tried to minimize that, and succeeded. Our culture has a built-in stability, you know, a negative feedback. To be sure, we must still take action about the home planet of those devils. Liberate their slave worlds and make certain they can't ever try afresh. But that shouldn't be difficult.

'As for you, I inquired very carefully on your behalf. Tervola remains in your family. The land and the people are as you remember.'

She closed her eyes, feeling the first thaw within herself. 'Now I can sleep,' she told him.

Remembering, she looked up with a touch of startlement. 'But you had a question for me, Ivalo?'

'Yes. All this time, I couldn't help wondering. Why you stayed with the enemy. You could have escaped. Did you know all the time how great a service you were going to do?'

Her own smile was astonishing to her. 'Well, I knew I couldn't be much use on Vaynamo,' she said. 'Could I? There was a

142

chance I could help on Chertkoi. But I wasn't being brave. The worst had already happened to me. Now I need only wait . . . a matter of months only, my time . . . and everything bad would be over. Whereas, well, if I'd escaped from the Second Expedition, I'd have lived most of my life in the shadow of the Third. Please don't make a fuss about me. I was actually an awful coward.'

His jaw dropped. 'You mean you knew we'd win? But you couldn't have! Everything pointed the other way!'

The nightmare was fading more rapidly than she had dared hope. She shook her head, still smiling, not triumphant but glad to speak the knowledge which had kept her alive. 'You're being unfair to our people. As unfair as the Chertkoians were. They thought that because we preferred social stability and room to breathe, we must be stagnant. They forgot you can have bigger adventures in, well, in the spirit, than in all the physical universe. We really did have a very powerful science and technology. It was oriented toward life, toward beautifying and improving instead of exploiting nature. But it wasn't less virile for that. Was it?'

'But we had no industry to speak of. We don't even now.'

'I wasn't counting on our factories, I said, but on our science. When you told me about that horrible virus weapon being suppressed, you confirmed my hopes. We aren't saints. Our government wouldn't have been quite so quick to get rid of the plague — would at least have tried to bluff with it — if there weren't something better in prospect. Wouldn't they?

'I couldn't even guess what our scientists might develop, given two generations which the enemy did not have. I did think they would probably have to use physics rather than biology. And why not? You can't have an advanced chemical, medical, genetic, ecological technology without knowing all the physics there is to know. Can you? Quantum theory explains mutations. But it also explains atomic reactions, or whatever they used in those new machines.

'Oh, yes, Ivalo, I felt sure we'd win. All I had to do myself was work to get us prisoners — especially me, to be quite honest — get us there at the victory.'

He looked at her with awe. Somehow that brought back the heaviness in her. *After all,* she thought . . . *sixty-two years. Tervola abides. But who will know me? I am going to be so much alone.*

Boots rang on metal. The young squad leader stepped back

143

in. 'That's that,' he said. His bleakness vanished and he edged closer to Elva, softly, almost timidly.

'I trust,' said Ivalo with a rich, growing pleasure in his voice, 'that my lady will permit me to visit her from time to time.'

'I hope you will,' she murmured.

'We temporal castaways are bound to be disorientated for a while,' he said. 'We must help each other. You, for example, may have some trouble adjusting to the fact that your son Hauki, the Freeholder of Tervola –'

'Hauki!' She sprang to her feet. The cabin blurred around her.

' – is now a vigorous elderly man who looks back on a most successful life,' said Ivalo. 'Which includes the begetting of Karlavi here.' Her grandson's strong hands closed about her own. 'Who in turn,' finished Ivalo, 'is the recent father of a bouncing baby boy named Hauki. And all your people are waiting to welcome you home.'